Ollie: Driverton 3
The Barrington Billionaires
Book 15

Ruth Cardello

Author Contact
website: RuthCardello.com
email: rcardello@ruthcardello.com
Facebook: Author Ruth Cardello
Twitter: RuthieCardello

Driverton's last standing bachelor has a chance to become more successful than anyone in his town has ever been, but he'll have to change more than his zip code to do it. One woman. One impossible decision. What will he choose?

Megan:

It's me again . . . waking, naked and alone, in the middle of a strange bed in God only knows which city.

The luxurious feel of the silk sheets is a delicious contrast to the rougher hands that spent hours exciting and exploring every inch of me. My skin is still flushed from the all-over brush of his short beard.

How do we keep returning to this place?

Our time together isn't planned, but just like a full moon is an unavoidable occurrence, all it takes is one look, one accidental touch for us to spontaneously combust.

He was right to leave Driverton. He had demons he needed to battle and opportunities he couldn't refuse. He's taking his shot at success, and I respect that. He needs to remain focused and I'm a distraction.

I should say no, but I fell for him back before he had money.

Back when all he had were the most beautiful eyes I'd ever seen.

The Barrington Billionaires:
Book 1: Always Mine
Book 2: Stolen Kisses
Book 3: Trade it All
Book 3.5: A Billionaire for Lexi (Novella)
Book 4: Let it Burn
Book 5: More than Love
Book 6: Forever Now
Book 7: Never Goodbye
Book 8: Reluctantly Alpha
Book 9: Reluctantly Rescued
Book 10: Reluctantly Romanced
Book 11: Loving a Landon
Book 12: Loathing a Landon
Book 13: Everette: Driverton 1
Book 14: Levi: Driverton 2
Book 15: Ollie: Driverton 3

Copyright

Ollie: Driverton 3
Copyright © 2024 by Ruth Cardello
Print Edition

ISBN eBook: 978-1-951888-77-0
ISBN Print: 978-1-951888-78-7

An Original work by Ruth Cardello

All Rights Reserved

This book or any portion thereof may not be reproduced or used in any manner whatsoever without the express written permission of the copyright owner except for the use of brief quotations in a book review.

This is a work of fiction. Any resemblance to actual persons, places, events, business establishments or locales is entirely coincidental.

Dedication

This book is dedicated to Dominic Corisi. He was the character who started my career. Some might argue that he's not real, but each time I write a scene with him in it, it's as if an old friend I adore has come for a visit. I chuckle at his arrogance. I smile with pride at his growth. Mostly, I'm grateful for the opportunity to have had the kind of career that has allowed me to grow with him.

Chapter One

Megan

A NIGHT OF *great sex shouldn't end with me waking naked and alone in the middle of a strange bed in God only knows which city.*

Yet, here I am.

The luxurious feel of silk sheets was a delicious contrast to the rougher hands that had spent hours exciting and exploring every inch of me. My skin was still flushed from the brush of his light beard, and the deep sleep that followed a multiple-orgasm romp left my body feeling refreshed and sated.

And my soul just a little sad.

I didn't want to wake up alone. I hated exploring a new hotel suite, fumbling around until I found what I needed, showering while trying to block out heated memories from the night before, and promising myself, again, this would be the last time.

I threw the comforter to the side and rolled to my feet,

pushing my tangled hair out of my eyes as I straightened. How do Ollie and I keep returning to this place?

I love him, but I'm not sure I like who he's becoming.

I padded to the bathroom. As I showered, I heard the rustling of someone in the other room. There was no need to wonder who it was. Ollie paid attention to details other men didn't. He knew I lived for weekends when I could slowly work my way through a pot of coffee, a stack of pancakes, and a steamy romance novel.

When I finished showering, the hotel staff would have set a table with coffee and pancakes—blueberry because they're my favorite. On one side, there would be a vase of flowers and a signed copy of whatever romance was topping the charts.

There'd be a dress I'd want to hate, but it would be beautiful, modest, and perfectly my taste. The shoes he'd have chosen to go with it would be classy but comfortable. All of it would fit as if made for me. I'd want to reject them, leave them behind with a note that said they weren't enough, but I'd wear them on my flight home because he'd bought them, and I wanted a piece of him with me.

He was giving me as much of himself as he had time for, but it wasn't enough. I knew what he was working toward, and at first, I thought we could make it work, but I needed more. Not more things. Not more gifts. I needed more of him.

I sighed and turned the water off before reaching for a fluffy, white robe. There was a time, not that long ago, when

I would have oohed and aahed over the expensive details woven throughout the high-priced world Ollie now lived in. It was nice. Everything smelled clean and fresh. People were attentive and helpful, but only because they were paid to be.

Honestly, I preferred visiting Driverton and sleeping in Ollie's room at his mother's house than . . .

You don't have to say it. I know. Sleeping in Ollie's old bed and hanging out with his mother is not helping me sort through my feelings for him. I need to have an honest conversation with him. I can't live like this.

The problem is, I'm so damn proud of him and the way he's battling for his future—he says ours, but I'm not sure I know him anymore.

He was right to leave Driverton. He had demons he needed to battle and opportunities he couldn't refuse. Taking his shot at success required all his time and focus. He was one hundred percent committed to not sliding back into being the man he'd been before he'd left, and I admire that.

There's just no room for me on his crusade to be successful. Flying out to wherever he is, whenever he has time for me, doesn't feel good anymore.

I should say no, but I've never been able to—not with him.

It's been like that since we first met.

Back before he had money.

Back when all he had was the most beautiful eyes I'd ever seen.

Chapter Two

Ollie

"Y OU MISSED EVERETTE'S birthday party," Levi said with more than a bit of judgment in his tone. Levi was my best friend, but he could also be a RPITA (Repetitive Pain in the Ass). It wasn't that I didn't love him or wasn't grateful to have someone who had always and would always have my back. I only wished he'd shut up about everything he thought I was doing wrong and how it might blow up in my face.

I glanced at my driver to see if he was listening, then decided it didn't matter. He was employed by Dominic Corisi, and that meant not only had he been vetted down to the fillings in his teeth, but he'd also been trained to be discreet. Nothing good happened to anyone who crossed the man who'd, unbelievable as it might sound, decided to mentor me. "I'm in the air and on my way to Singapore. I told you this."

"If you have time to fly Megan out to you, you have time

to fly your ass home now and then."

My irritation spilled over. "I'm not having this conversation. You know how tight my schedule is."

"This isn't you, Ollie. You don't need to jump every time Dominic snaps his fingers."

"Did you call to insult me, or can I help you with something?"

"I'm worried about you."

"Based on nothing. Dominic has done everything he promised he would. He guided me toward startups with cutting-edge technology. He taught me how to buy them out, optimize their market, and double my investment by selling their product to those unwilling to fight for it in the trenches. I'm learning so much from him. Why would I say no to him when all he wants is for me to repay him the money he invested and be his next success story?"

"Are you sure that's all he wants?"

"And this is why I haven't come home. Do you know who believes in me more than you? Complete strangers. When I walk into a room and introduce myself for the first time, no one doubts that I'm capable of closing a deal."

"But why? Why did he choose you?"

That question cut deep. I shouldn't have to explain to my best friend why I was good enough. And, God, not every time we talked. "Dominic surrounds himself with people who have proven track records of loyalty and good character. Clay said a lot of great things about me to him and he decided I was worth his time. He doesn't care that I've been to rehab. The head of his security, Marc Stone, struggled with alcohol for a while. Past mistakes don't matter to him—performance and commitment do. And I'm achieving every goal he sets for me. It's only for six months. After that, I'll attend every birthday party."

"Bradford thinks—"

"Bradford has never liked me."

"That's not true. He stepped up when you needed him."

I took a moment to look out the window. No one liked to be reminded of their weakest moments, but I did owe Bradford for sending me to Boston and arranging for people to lift me up when I was at my lowest. "I will always be grateful for that and soon I'll be able to pay that kindness forward—a hundredfold."

"I know how tempting money and success must be, but—"

I laughed without humor at that. "Did you turn down the money Dominic offered for the island resort your parents left you?" We both knew he didn't. "Or is Dominic only okay to associate with when it puts millions in *your* pocket?"

Neither of us said anything for several minutes. Finally, in a quiet tone, he said, "Things are just changing so fast, I don't like it."

That was something I could understand. "But not forever. I'm closing a deal in Singapore that could allow me to pay back Dominic a month early. I'm so close. And after I pay him back, everything else I make is mine. That was the deal. After that, I can set my own schedule and choose my own jobs. All of this running around is temporary."

After a pause, Levi asked, "Where did you leave Megan this time?"

"Not on the side of the road. She's waking up in a five-star hotel in San Francisco. There's a private jet at her disposal to fly her home or back to Driverton or wherever she wants to go. So before you try to convince me I'm not treating her right, tell me, would I be doing more for her if I still owned Little Willie's and was drowning in debt? Were you and I better people when Everette was rolling us out of the back of his truck and carrying our passed-out asses to our porches?"

He sighed. "No."

"Okay, then stop worrying. I've got this."

"Do something for me."

"Anything."

"If this goes sideways, swear you'll come home, and we'll fix it together."

"Nothing will go wrong, but, okay, I swear."

Chapter Three

Dominic Corisi

Dominic Corisi was in his Boston office reading over an update from his South American team when he looked up and spotted the head of his security team seated in the chair before his desk. He didn't ask her how she got there unnoticed. Alethea's stealthiness and cunning were top-notch and something she prided herself on. Before meeting Dominic, she'd made her fortune by circumventing the security systems of private and public entities, then offering her services to rectify the issues. Her curiosity was insatiable, and the global informant network she'd built was unnerving. There was no one better at uncovering what others wanted to remain hidden, and that was why she held an honored position on Dominic's team. More importantly, her loyalty was why she was among the few people he considered not just a friend but part of his family.

The smooth smile she shot him was pure trouble. Dominic leaned back in his chair and forcefully drummed his fingers on the desk. "If this is about Judy, the answer is no. You know my feelings about her not wanting a security detail at college. She can pretend to be whoever she wants to be, but she's still my daughter and I will keep her safe."

Alethea crossed one leg over the other and smoothed the material of her pants leg in a move he recognized as a tell that she was uncertain. "I'm in full agreement, which is why our people are still there, but less obvious. I now have more than one of her professors on payroll."

"Good."

"This isn't about her."

The only time Alethea hedged was when she knew she was overstepping. Dominic arched an eyebrow and waited.

She cleared her throat. "We've worked together for a long time."

No way was she quitting. If there was one thing Dominic made sure of, it was that the people who were loyal to him were more successful than they could have become on their own. So what did she want? If it was a change of assignment due to another pregnancy or something personal, there was no need for her to dance around the request. She had to know he was as much on her team as she was on his. "What is this about?"

"Ollie Williams."

A corner of Dominic's mouth curled in amused acknowledgment of her skill. There was no one Dominic loved more than his wife, Abby, but there was no one who saw through him better than Alethea. His only surprise was that it had taken her this long to bring Ollie up. "Yes?"

"He is by far not the first relatively unknown person I've seen you help over the years. So, I understand why, to others, it may appear that your motive in helping him is completely altruistic."

"But you don't think it is?" He was toying with her and they both knew it. It amazed him sometimes how even those closest to him still tread carefully when it came to confronting him. *Am I that bad?* He viewed himself as becoming more supportive and protective over the years. "Whatever it is, just say it, Alethea."

"You know that both Marc and I would take a bullet for you."

Dominic nodded. He'd do the same for them.

She continued, "I'd prefer if that doesn't happen over something . . ."

"Something . . . ?" he countered.

Slowly, as if it weren't her first choice of response, she said, "Unnecessarily dangerous?"

"Go on."

She took a moment. "My instincts tell me that you have plans for Williams that may incur the wrath of someone with a propensity toward violence on a level we haven't faced in years."

Bradford Wilson. Dominic didn't say his name aloud because they both knew who she was referring to. "And if I do?"

"Of course I would ensure that we have whatever intel necessary to cripple him financially as well as isolate him from whoever might come to his defense."

"Of course."

"But some of those who would side with him are within your inner circle."

"I'm aware of his affiliation with the Barringtons."

"Ian Barrington in particular."

"Yes."

"Sophie Barrington has also taken a personal interest in Ollie. So, even if we neutralized the main threat, there would be substantial fallout."

"Do you believe I couldn't handle the disapproval of any of the Barringtons?"

"No, but I feel I wouldn't be your friend if I didn't ask you to consider if whatever you're doing is worth it."

It was a valid question and asked with Dominic's best interest at heart, so he tolerated it. "It is."

She folded and unfolded her hands on her lap. "I could prepare on my side better if I knew your plans for Williams."

Dominic's eyes narrowed.

She added, "Or your reasoning. I've investigated Williams and the people of Driverton extensively. He was dealt a tough hand, but many of them were and they seem to have found a way to rise above challenges. And, maybe because I know my husband struggled with alcohol after he left the

Marines, I want to see Williams succeed. If your plans for him aren't in his best interest, you should reconsider moving forward with them."

Taking a moment to weigh her words, Dominic stood and walked to look out the floor-to-ceiling window of his office. "How do you know you are loyal if that loyalty has never been tested?"

"Me?" she rose to her feet.

"Anyone." He looked out over the skyline of Boston. "How does a person know what they value unless they've been offered a chance at something different and have to choose?"

"You're testing Williams's integrity? By what? By making him successful then taking it away?" Her voice lowered as she realized she'd answered her own question. "Dominic, you're not God."

Dominic laughed without humor. "No one has ever confused me with him. In fact, it's always quite the opposite."

"Then why do this? What's the endgame?"

"I owe Wilson a favor."

Alethea gasped. "I respectfully must say I don't see how this will be seen as anything to him outside of an act of war against people Bradford considers under his protection."

"He may believe that at first. But in the end, I will have repaid him twofold. He'll know for certain if Williams deserves his protection, and I'll have helped him cement a relationship with someone he undervalues but shouldn't."

"Clay Landon."

"Every Batman needs a Robin."

Alethea rolled her eyes. "They're already friends."

"No, they're associates with a rocky history. I was asked to help them smooth out their issues."

"Who? Who asked you?"

Dominic turned toward Alethea and frowned. "Katie Berber." After a moment, he added, "She asked me to help Bradford and Clay see past their differences and value each other. Well, she said she *wanted* to ask me to, but that some things would be impossible even for a man like me." Alethea choked on what sounded to Dominic like a laugh. He shot her a glare. "Is that amusing to you?"

"No. No, this information just gave me a deeper appreciation of Katie. That's exactly how to get *you* to do something. I knew there was a reason I liked her."

He rose to his full height, gray eyes flashing with irritation. "If you're suggesting that my plan was actually hers..."

This time Alethea laughed aloud. "I can guarantee that her idea of you helping Bradford and Clay become friends bore no resemblance to your current strategy."

Dominic rolled his shoulders back dismissively. "It's a solid plan."

"That could get one of us killed if it goes wrong."

"I can handle Bradford."

Alethea shook her head. "I was referring to Abby. She

won't be happy with any of us if she gets wind of this."

"I don't keep secrets from her, but it's sometimes best to delay when she receives information. After Ollie has proven himself, or not, and Bradford and Clay are on the same team, I'll explain to her why I decided to become involved at all. If Bradford and Clay can't resolve their issues, they'll tear that town apart. All I'm doing is stopping that from happening."

"I can't endorse this as a good idea."

He pinned her with his gaze. "But you can support it and keep the details of it between us."

"Yes." Her chin rose. "You've always had my back even when I was wrong. I'll do everything I can to keep this from derailing, but if this puts me back on Abby's shitlist . . ."

"It won't because she'll only hear about it after it's done."

"Yeah," Alethea swallowed visibly. "That always works out well."

Chapter Four

Megan

Ten months earlier

Back when all he had were the most beautiful eyes I'd ever seen . . .

L*ORD, I WISH I were sober.* There was a real possibility my assessment of the man who was guiding me across a lawn and through what could only be described as a redneck party was faulty. Or was it a picnic? It was difficult to say. We wove through countless people sitting on blankets, eating at fold-up tables, or lounging on lawn chairs. I really shouldn't have had that second bottle of champagne, but how often does a person get to ride in a luxury helicopter while a hunk of a man serves unlimited alcohol?

"And he was hot."

"Who?" the man who was guiding me asked.

"The guy on the helicopter." I stifled a burp and made a face as the taste of it filled my mouth. "I didn't mean to say that out loud. I know men don't like to hear about other men."

"No offense taken." He chuckled and dipped his head closer. "Although the drunker you sound, the less stock I'm putting into your claim that I have beautiful eyes. Can you even see them?"

I paused and looked up into the darkest, brownest eyes I'd ever seen. "I would kill to have your eyelashes. They're so long."

He smiled and encouraged me to keep walking. "Can't say I've ever gotten that compliment, so thanks."

"Where are we going?" He may have told me, but damned if I could remember.

"You, my friend, are a code purple. Levi's getting you coffee. I'll get you to the furthest empty table I can find, and we'll sober you up."

"Before anyone notices? Good."

"Well, the belch you let out when you first landed did carry across the crowd, but old Mrs. McDonald has been known to let out a similar sound whenever she eats chili so . . ."

"Champagne is so gassy." The relief I felt when he stopped at a table and held out a chair for me was immeasurable. It would have been nice, though, to be warned that, since the chair was on grass, plopping down on it wasn't a good idea. Two of the legs sank into the soft earth beneath it and I would have slid to the ground if my brown-eyed friend hadn't swooped in to save me. He placed me back on the chair, righted it, then pulled up a chair beside me.

The world spun and for a moment I thought I might hurl. He must have seen the distress in my eyes because he scooted his chair back about a foot. "Just breathe," he advised.

"Is that something people forget to do?" I asked in what I hoped was a witty tone.

He chuckled. "I have no idea. Just seemed like a better thing to say than please don't vomit on my lap."

That had me laughing as well. I brought a hand to my mouth as I admitted, "I thought I might."

"I know."

"I don't drink."

"The evidence does not support that claim."

I laughed again. "Normandy. Sorry, normally. Normally, I don't drink." I sighed wistfully. "But how could I say no when a hunky god of a man topped off my glass after every sip?" I searched the man's eyes beside me. "He was a gift from Shelby. It would have been rude not to drink what he offered me."

"A crime, really."

"Exactly," I leaned toward Mr. Brown Eyes and laid a hand on his thigh. "And it's probably illegal to turn down free champagne."

"Most definitely."

"Not that I would do anything inappro-diate. *Inaprolliate.*" I hiccupped and straightened, holding up a finger in a request for him to wait a moment. "I can say it. Don't say it for me. In-ap-pro-priate." Hopping with excitement, I clapped my hands together. "I knew I could do it."

"I had faith in you and your ability."

Bringing a hand to my heart, I said, "You did? That is the sweetest thing to say."

Another man appeared with a Styrofoam cup he almost handed to me, but Mr. Brown Eyes intercepted it and asked, "Is it hot?"

The other man shrugged.

Mr. Brown Eyes sipped from the cup first. "Let's give it a moment to cool before we give it to her. She's a little wasted right now and would probably guzzle it."

I pointed at Mr. Brown Eyes as I remembered something. "Your name is Ollie. I'm good with names. I trained myself to associate a person, a name, and an image when I meet someone. I saw a collie in my head. A brown-eyed collie. Ollie."

He nodded. "I've been associated with worse."

I looked over the man beside him. "You're a pair of jeans."

His smile was kind. "Levi."

Pleased with myself I sat back in my chair and almost toppled over again.

"Easy there," Ollie said, steadying my chair and, this time, keeping a hand on the back of it.

Levi said, "Good news? Everette's girlfriend can't judge us for drinking if this is an example of her friends."

I sat up straighter at that and waved a finger at him. "I don't drink." The slur of my words stole all credibility from my claim. Neither man corrected me.

"What do you think of Shelby?" Ollie asked.

"She's my best friend," I said confidently. "I love her."

With a smile in those beautiful eyes of his, Ollie said, "Pipe down there, Turtle Lady. I was asking Levi."

Levi looked across the lawn to where Shelby and Everette were gazing into each other's eyes like lovers reunited after a war.

Before he had a chance to answer, I said, "If either of you say a negative thing about my friend, I will sock you both in the nose."

Ollie laughed. "This one is a firecracker."

"But loyal," Levi added.

They both looked at me in approval. I'd come to Driverton as moral support for Shelby, who'd wanted to meet up with Everette after their breakup. Getting drunk hadn't been the plan, but luckily she didn't appear to need me anymore.

Sober me would have been concerned that I was in the care of two men I'd never met before. Nothing about the situation felt dangerous, though. They weren't flirting with me. In fact, although I'd never had a sibling, they were giving off big brother vibes. I looked back and forth between them, then asked, "How do you know I like turtles?"

Ollie exchanged a look with Levi then me. "I'm either psychic, or Shelby threatened to feed my testicles to your pet turtle if I tried anything with you."

That filled me with delight. "I do have a turtle and I love to use that threat."

He nodded with a smile. "Are you just as bold when you're sober?"

My shoulders slumped a bit and I sighed. "People don't call me bold. I'm nice. I'm the kind of person who'll use my vacation days to go with you to visit your boyfriend if you don't feel like you could go alone. I'm cute. Sweet. Easy to get along with. Not bold."

Whatever either of them would have responded to that was lost when Shelby and Everette joined us. Levi vacated his seat so Shelby could sit beside me. She looked me over then asked, "How are you feeling? You look a little green."

"I've been better." Looking up at Everette, I smiled. "I knew you'd be happy to see her."

He was an adorable giant. "Thank you for convincing her to come. I owe you—big."

"Just be good to her," I said.

"I will," he promised.

Everette's dog, Tyr, came bounding up and barked at him. Everette said, "He probably wants water. I'll be right back."

Ollie stood. "I'll go with you."

"Wait for me," Levi said and suddenly Shelby and I were alone.

I said, "I can't believe the whole town came out to meet you. You belong here with Everette."

Her enthusiasm held more caution, but I understood because she'd experienced a significant loss not too long ago. It would take time for her to heal from that. "I wouldn't have come if you hadn't come with me," she admitted quietly.

I took one of her hands in mine. "Yes, you would have. Eventually. You're stronger than you know."

She gave my hand a squeeze. "And damn lucky to have a friend like you."

"Well, duh. I always tell you that."

We shared a laugh.

After blinking a few times quickly, she said, "I want this to work out, Megan. I want it so badly."

"Then be brave enough to let it happen."

"Those are some wise words there."

"Yep, who knew champagne would turn me into fucking Socrates."

We laughed again.

The expression on Shelby's face changed and her eyes rounded. I turned to see what she could be worried about. A petite older woman was striding toward us. "I know who that is," Shelby said in a hushed tone.

"Who?" I answered in a whisper.

"Ollie's mother."

"Is she scary? Why are you whispering?" I asked.

The woman was beside the table before Shelby responded. She introduced herself as Mrs. Williams. Shelby rose to her feet to greet her. I thought it was best that I didn't just in case my legs were as unstable as my chair was.

Mrs. Williams took both of Shelby's hands in hers. "I've heard so much about you."

"Same," Shelby said nervously.

"Our Everette has already given you his heart. I hope you treat it like the treasure it is."

"I will."

"I believe you," the older woman said before releasing Shelby's hands and turning her attention to me. "And who is this?"

"Mrs. Williams," Shelby said, "this is my very best friend in the world, Megan Gassett."

I nodded rather than say anything that might reveal how drunk I was.

"It's nice to meet you, Megan," Mrs. William said.

I nodded again.

"Shy?" she asked.

"Wasted," I answered without thinking, then snapped my mouth shut and looked away.

"Interesting." Somehow Mrs. Williams put an entire judgmental lecture into that one word.

Shelby rushed to explain that it was her fault because she'd wanted to make the flight over special for me so she'd requested food and drinks to be served.

Mrs. Williams cut in. "Doesn't matter what a person is served, it only matters what they choose to indulge in. First impressions are important, Miss Gassett. So is your health. Or are neither of those important to you?"

"I don't know a lot about alcohol," I said slowly, careful not to slur my words. "But my mother taught me the art of getting to know a person before passing judgment on them."

Probably only because I was still buzzed beyond being sensible, the glare Mrs. Williams shot me rolled off my back like water off a duck. Some people go through life arguing with everyone and worrying about what other people think of them. I'd been born much more chill than that. I liked most people and most people liked me.

I was selective about who I called a friend, and exclusive when it came to calling anyone more than that, but I couldn't remember the last person I'd actively disliked. If I didn't care for someone, I tended to avoid them, but I didn't carry around any negative feelings toward them.

So I smiled in response to Mrs. William's glare.

And her huff.

And the tsk she made as she shook her head.

I smiled and didn't interrupt Shelby as she told Mrs. Williams about how long we'd been friends, how I'd been there for her every step of the way, and that no one should base their entire opinion of anyone on a first impression. Hopefully, there'd be plenty of time for us to all get to know each other since we'd be staying in town for a few days.

"Only a few days?" Mrs. Williams asked, suddenly looking concerned rather than offended.

"I have to get back to my job," I said.

"What do you do?" She pinned me with a look.

"I work in customer service for a commercial airline."

Mrs. Williams's eyes narrowed. "You like it?"

I shrugged. "I like helping people and I've been there long enough that my supervisor allows me flexibility when it comes to using my vacation time, so . . . I guess?"

In a tentative voice, Shelby said, "I'm hoping if I end up liking Driverton, Megan might as well."

That had Mrs. Williams's eyebrows rising to meet her hairline. "Is that a possibility?"

I looked to Shelby for help. When she didn't provide any, I said, "I know next to nothing about Driverton except what Everette has claimed it is. If it's the wonderful place he's described and Shelby moves here, I'd consider it."

Mrs. Williams smiled in my direction for the first time, but I couldn't tell if that meant she liked me or not. "Well, then of course, the two of you are welcome to stay at my home while you're here. Driverton doesn't have hotels nearby and just about everyone who comes through stays in my spare rooms."

The way Shelby's mouth opened and closed like a fish

out of water suggested she hadn't thought that far ahead. "Everette and I haven't talked about that yet . . ."

"No one will bat an eye if you stay with me. Like I said, I'm the unofficial bed and breakfast. Your other choice is to stay with Everette's family. Not too many bedrooms over there, though. Up to you, if you want to put one of them . . ." She looked at me. "Two of them out of their beds and onto couches."

"Oh, no, I'd never do that," Shelby said. "If you're okay with us staying with you, we'd love to."

I reached for the coffee I hadn't yet sampled and took a healthy, and thankfully only lukewarm, gulp of it. "I'm Shelby's wingwoman, so count me in for wherever she goes."

Chin high, Mrs. Williams said, "I don't charge anyone, but I do ask that they help out around the place." Her eyes narrowed again as she looked at me. "Can you cook?"

A smile spread across my face. "Not only can I, but I love to. I was born in the wrong generation because I'd love to be a round older woman, serving up bowls of pasta with meatballs the size of your head. If your fridge has more than three ingredients, I can make a meal."

"If that's true, would you consider helping out at our family's restaurant a few times while you're here?"

"Did I just get hired?" I asked with a laugh.

"For a job that doesn't pay," she countered with a bit of challenge in her eyes.

"My favorite kind," I parried back. Then, just because

she seemed to be softening toward me, I leaned on one elbow and winked up at her. "I should find something to do since I am a third wheel." In a more serious tone, I nodded to Shelby. "I don't mind. I know you need time to make sure you feel safe here. I got you."

Shelby wrapped her arms around me and gave me a tight hug before straightening, sniffing, and facing Mrs. Williams again. "You see why she's my best friend?"

Mrs. Williams nodded, looking back and forth at both of us. "I do."

Chapter Five

Ollie

MORNING CAME TOO early. The light searing through my closed eyelids meant my mother had entered my room, tried to wake me, then decided to let the sun do what she couldn't. I groaned, stretched, and rolled to my feet.

Thank God my cousin Katie had the morning shift at Little Willie's because there was no way in hell I'd be heading to my family's restaurant before noon. I shot off a text to Katie saying as much. She sent me a string of emojis I'm certain were meant to be insulting but the lone brain cell that had survived a night of hard partying wasn't up to translating anything. If Katie was answering with anything but an excuse, it meant she was there and already working.

As I padded to the hallway bathroom in my boxers, I read a text from Levi asking me to drive him to get his truck.

From where? I texted. I remembered leaving the *Welcome to Driverton* gathering and heading out of town with Levi. There was the first bar. A second bar. I flexed one of my hands. Maybe a fight? My face wasn't sore and a quick glance down at my bare chest confirmed I was unhurt, still sporting morning wood, but I took that as another good sign. There was at least one piece of me that was ready to meet the day.

You remember the brunette? She invited us back to her place to party with her friends. *Oh, yeah.* **We left my truck there.**

Okay. Give me thirty minutes. *We called Cooper to pick us up because we were both too drunk to drive. Now I remember.*

I was lowering the phone when I bumped into someone. "Sorry," I mumbled, continuing to walk past.

"That's okay," a soft female voice answered and I froze. I knew that voice. Turning so I could confirm she was who I thought she was, I smiled. "Morning, Turtle Lady."

She was all eyes for a moment, and I couldn't blame her. Fresh from bed was not my best look. My hair would be sticking out in all directions. A smirk pulled at my lips when her gaze dipped low enough to take in the part of me that was tenting my boxers. As if realizing what she'd been caught doing, her eyes flew up to mine and her face went bright red. "Sorry. I was just leaving the bathroom."

"Perfect timing. That's where I'm heading." Nothing about the wreck I must have been stopped me from winking at her and saying, "Or maybe I should have gotten up sooner and met you there. You're adorable." She was. Shorter than my type and pleasantly curvy, she looked like someone's little housewife in her sleeveless wrap-around dress and sandals.

Her hair flowed in waves past her shoulders and overlong bangs framed her face. Just enough makeup to make her eyes pop. She was definitely a cut above any woman I'd ever met. I leaned closer. She even smelled good. Perfection.

Her mouth rounded in surprise then quickly changed to amusement. "That's a lot of swagger for a man with a hickey on his neck. I didn't know people still did that."

A memory of the woman a substantial amount of alcohol had made seem like a good idea just a few hours earlier came back to me and I winced. Not every drunken decision held up to scrutiny the next day. "Welcome to Driverton," was the best response I could come up with.

She wrinkled her nose at me as if I smelled, effectively killing my erection. I shrugged. Not only did women like her not visit my hometown—but Driverton also had nothing to tempt her to stay. I could flirt with her, but considering she was the friend of Everette's new love, it was best to leave it at that.

I'd started to turn away from her when she said, "Hey, quick question . . ."

"Yes?"

"Your mother asked if I'd cook up a few things for your restaurant. I want to make something people would like. What do you suggest?"

I could think of several things I'd like from her and none of it included cooking, but her expression was so earnest I stomped those thoughts out of my head. "We keep the menu simple. Pasta. Soups. Sandwiches. If possible, make enough for people to have some to take home. My mother can show you where we keep the containers to place in the fridge near the door."

She nodded. "Shelby told me about Little Willie's and how it's the heart of Driverton."

"I wouldn't say that."

"She said people pay when they can, bring their own food when they can't, and often wash their own dishes. The extra food you put in the fridge, is that for people to take if they need it? For no charge?"

"Yes."

"How does Little Willie's stay open?"

Her question made me feel more exposed than being barely clothed did. "It just does." When she looked up at me with an expectation of me saying more, I added, "My father opened it because there was a need for a place for locals to gather. When he died, he left it to me. All I'm doing is keeping it open."

"That can't be easy."

"It is what it is."

We stood there in some weird moment outside of time. I was reasonably attractive and was used to women giving me a certain look when they were interested, but this felt different. Megan wasn't ogling me like a dirty indulgence she was considering. Nor was there a hint of judgment in her eyes. No, she was looking past my reputation and bravado and into my soul. I felt seen but in an uncomfortable way.

"Well, I think what you do is remarkable. The world needs more places where people can go when in need and still contribute."

"The health department wouldn't agree, but the inspector went to school with me, and he knows I know where he lives."

She smiled. "Or he admires you. I know I do."

Emotion clogged my throat. No one, not my friends, not the people I'd grown up with, not even my mother had ever said they admired me. Her words hit me hard, and I stepped back. "Give me time, I'll change that."

She looked about to say something I knew I didn't want to hear, so I did what my instincts told me to, and walked away.

Safely inside the bathroom, I shed my boxers, emptied my bladder, and turned on the shower. The sting of the hot water wasn't enough to stop me from imagining Megan standing right where I was, soaping up that hot little body of hers. I breathed in and the scent of some flowery shampoo teased my senses.

How long was she staying? A few days? I could keep my dick in my pants that long. My thoughts filled with images of her standing in front of me again. Would her lips taste as sweet as they looked? What would she have done had I hauled her to me, slid my hands beneath the hem of her dress and up the sides of her thighs? I bet she wore cotton panties that matched her bra. Pink. Or tan. I imagined running my hand across the front of them, pleased at how their thin material would betray how excited she was.

Taking my cock in my hand, I imagined touching her instead. Right there in the hallway, I'd fuck her mouth with my tongue while my fingers pushed all barriers between them and her sex aside. As I pumped my hand up and down on my shaft, I imagined dipping a finger inside her, then bringing it to my mouth for a taste of what I'd feast on later.

When I had her moaning and begging for me not to stop, only then would I turn her around so she could brace herself against the shower wall. I'd grab a handful of her hair and arch her backward while I drove my cock into her again and again. So deep. So fucking hard she'd forget the name of any man before me. Relentlessly, I'd pound into her, until . . . until . . .

Alone in the shower, I came with a groan and a shudder. Not bad. Better than the sex I could barely remember from the night before. Not as good as having Megan actually there would have been, but since there was zero chance of that happening, it was better than nothing. After washing down, I turned off the water, grabbed a towel from the closet, slung it around my hips, tossed my boxers in the hamper, and padded back toward my room.

Just another day.

Life in Driverton wasn't anything to brag about, but it wasn't so bad. I had good friends, a roof over my head, and a mother who loved me even when I tested her very last nerve. Prior to my father's death a couple years back, I hadn't understood how much his generosity with the community had cost him—cost us. Little Willie's operated in the red and my father had left his bank accounts in the same condition.

On his deathbed, I'd promised him two things: One, that I'd make sure his vision continued. That's what he considered Little Willie's—not a restaurant, but just as Megan had said, he'd seen it as something Driverton needed. My second promise was a harder one to keep. He didn't want my mother to ever know the condition he'd left his finances in. He spouted some end-of-life stupid fear that she would think he chose the well-being of our community over caring for her, and he needed her to never doubt his love for her.

So, as far as my mother was concerned, Little Willie's had been financially profitable until I took over. She didn't know the side hustles I worked online and out of town to bring in income each month to cover not only our bills but a backlog of debt my father had run up.

And I'd never tell her.

My father's voice echoed in my head, "It's better to do the right thing and be poorly perceived than to be celebrated and know you don't deserve it."

For that reason, I let my mother think I was always too tired from getting drunk. Drinking didn't help my situation, but honestly, especially lately, it was the one thing I did for myself.

Drunk me was happy and free.

If remaining in that state 24/7 wouldn't have broken both of my promises to my father, I would have gladly chosen it as often as I could afford to. Although there wasn't much I regretted, there was also nothing for me to look forward to.

Even with the influx of some wealthy people into our town, not too much changed in Driverton and not everyone trusted the newcomers. I was still on the fence. They seemed like nice enough people, but they also had a lot of big ideas for a town as small as Driverton.

Everette claimed training with Bradford had been life-changing. There was no denying Everette looked healthy as fuck and seemed happier than I'd ever seen him. For that reason alone, Katie, Levi, and I were willing to give it a shot.

Not today.

Not while I feel like shit.

But soon.

Chapter Six

>>>><<<<

Megan

WHEN I ENTERED the kitchen Shelby was scrambling eggs and Mrs. Williams was buttering toast. Without hesitation, I asked, "How can I help?"

"The glasses are in that cabinet. You could pour orange juice for anyone who wants some," Mrs. Williams responded.

Cheeks still flushed from my hallway meet-up, I hurried to occupy myself. "Three or four?" Would Ollie join us? Did it matter if he did? It shouldn't.

My parents, although nice enough people, had been both strict and overprotective. I imagined their horror if I told them I was the slightest bit attracted to a man who not only still lived with his mother but was also, apparently, a drinker. My mother didn't care which sex I decided to partner with as long as the person was able to support me if I decided to stay home, as she had, to raise the grandchildren she was eager for. My father was a bit more easygoing, but as someone who'd paid for his own college degree and worked two jobs to buy a house for my mother, he had no patience for anyone he considered unmotivated. Thankfully I'd stopped requiring their approval on many things years ago. I love them, but in more than small doses, they drove me a little crazy. They probably felt the same way about me. My mother liked to joke that I was sugar-coated defiance. All that meant was that I would politely listen to opposition to one of my ideas, usually keep my opinion to myself, then smile and go off and do whatever it was I was going to do before the lecture.

That kind of confidence didn't come from believing I knew more than others but from knowing myself. Sure, I made mistakes, but I woke up every day with the goal of being a good person who made the world a better place, even if it was only in the smallest of ways. So, I smiled at people when they growled at me. I picked up litter others dropped and agreed to spend my vacation days in a small town in the middle of nowhere, cooking for strangers.

Some might have considered me naïve, but it wasn't that I didn't see the ugliness in the world—*oh, I did.* When Shelby had lost both of her parents to a home invasion gone bad, it had devastated both of us.

She'd shut down, withdrawn, and considered giving up. How could life hold any meaning when horrific things happened and everyone but the directly affected continued going on?

I didn't have the answer to that question, but I stuck by her while she wrestled with it. Sometimes, that's all a person can do. Was Everette the right man for her? Only time would tell, but I'd be right there by her side, just as she'd always been there for me. That last thought had me smiling as I turned toward Mrs. Williams and waited for her response.

She looked me over with an intensity that made me a little uncomfortable, but I didn't let that dim my smile. I wasn't there to win her over and she'd either like me or she wouldn't. All I could do was be myself. "Three," she said. "If I know my son, he'll slip out the back door rather than face me this morning."

I couldn't blame him. She looked like someone with a lot to say and none of it positive. I felt compelled to defend him. "Your son was very nice to me yesterday."

She looked me over again. "Is that why you're all dressed up for a date with the kitchen?"

I could have gotten defensive, but where would that have gotten us? Her beef wasn't with me. Instead, empty glass in each hand, I raised my arms and said, "This is what happens when you pack for the trip and not the destination. Did you see the helicopter we arrived in? It was so fancy I didn't even think about bringing jeans. Tomorrow's outfit is a flowered version of this."

Shelby's shoulders shook with a laugh she was holding back. If we were the same size, I would have suggested we switch wardrobes. She'd gone the cautious, casual route. Unfortunately, she had a good six inches on me and had always been thinner.

"Would you like an apron?" Mrs. Williams asked somewhat grudgingly.

"I'd love one." After slipping one over my head, I went to the fridge to retrieve the orange juice. While filling the glasses, an idea came to me. "You have a pork roast. My mother makes the best pulled pork. If we can get more of it and you have the ingredients I need, I could make a large batch. It's an easy meal to take away and could be used as a staple in tacos, chili, meatloaf, sandwiches... my mother even baked leftovers into corn muffins.

Shelby lit up at my suggestion. "It really is amazing. Everette and I can make a store run for everything you'd need."

"You don't have to—"

Shelby cut off Mrs. Williams. "Please, it would make me feel better about accepting the generosity you've shown us by letting us stay here."

"Put that way, how could I say no?" After inhaling deeply, Mrs. Williams said, "I've been known to make a decent pulled pork, myself."

I smiled because my mother could also be territorial about her kitchen. "I'll happily use either recipe. Or we can compare and blend them; see if we come up with something even better."

Mrs. Williams stared me down. "You think you can improve on *my* pulled pork?" She did not look pleased with the idea.

My superpower, if I had one at all, was my unflappable belief that most people didn't want to be confrontational. They'd flex and posture in the face of the unknown, but if shown only positivity and acceptance, they'd soften. Most people—not all. Some, like my parents, couldn't lower their guard, not even around the people closest to them. They chose structure and fear instead of trust and couldn't understand that they didn't have to live that way. All their rules, all the judgments they held to, didn't keep them safe . . . just isolated and angry.

My grandmother, one of the wisest people I'd ever known, and someone I still missed every single day, even though she'd been gone for nearly five years, used to say, "Always give a person a chance to show you who they are." I didn't understand what that meant when I was a child, but the older I got the more it made sense. Getting to know a person took time and patience. It often involved looking past their "gatekeeper personality." That was another term my grandmother had used that took me time to understand.

A gatekeeper personality is what a person presents to others until they feel comfortable enough to reveal more. It's why someone who's been hurt might sound fearless. Or why a lonely person might claim to dislike everyone. With me, it meant people who didn't know me well often missed how loyal I was and how deliberate my decisions were. While under the strict rules of my parents, I'd had plenty of time to imagine what I'd do when I was finally free to.

Mrs. Williams probably saw me as carefree and easygoing. *That might be all she ever knows of me.*

Not everyone who comes into our life is supposed to enter our hearts as well.

Access past the gatekeeper is a privilege not everyone deserves.

Chapter Seven

Ollie

IT WAS EARLY afternoon when I strolled into Little Willie's with Levi. My cousin Katie rolled her eyes at us and looked down at the nonexistent watch on her wrist. I held up two fingers to her which was code for, "Yeah, yeah, bring over two beers."

As soon as we were seated at our usual table, I lowered my voice and said, "Thanks for lending me a hand at the Baxter place. I could have put up the sheetrock myself, but banging that out today will move the project along faster. Building the addition to his house is really helping me get ahead. Hell, this month I was able to pay the electricity and oil bills for both Little Willie's and my mother's house. That's rare."

Levi shrugged. "Anytime. Thanks for taking me to get my truck."

Katie delivered two beers as well as two pulled-pork sandwiches with fries. She might not be happy that I wasn't there to help with the lunch shift, but the Baxter job was the only reason I'd be able to pay her. She knew the financial situation my father had left Little Willie's in because for the first few weeks after his death I hadn't been able to pay her. What made Katie not only a good cousin, but also a solid human being was how she'd continued to come to work anyway—helping me keep both of my promises to my father.

Despite how many tables were full, Katie sat with us. "So, you two were either at a brothel or the Baxter's place."

I shot her a glare. "If that's your way of saying we're sweaty and look like shit, you can go find a table to clear. I'm here for lunch, then I'll be painting well into the night."

Levi took a bite of his sandwich and with his mouth full, mumbled, "This is awesome. Did you make it, Katie?"

She shook her head. "It's really good, isn't it? I like Shelby well enough, but Everette might have chosen wrong between her and her friend. Megan sure can cook. She's so sweet too. And funny. Aunt Reana was introducing her around like she was an old friend in town for a visit. Megan's even driving your mom's car. Watch out or you'll wake up married to her, Ollie. Your mother's already in love."

I didn't take too much of what Katie said seriously since one of her favorite pastimes was to give me shit. Instead, I homed in on what mattered. "My mother was here? Did she ask where I was?"

"No, just assumed you were off somewhere day-drinking."

A memory of drunk Megan came back to me and I smiled. Had she not been so gone, I might have hung around to talk to her. She was extremely . . . likable. Rather than giving in to the temptation to scour the room to see if she was still there, I chugged down half my beer. "We *did* stop for a round on our way back, but only to do our part to support the local economy."

Katie pursed her lips. "Do you have anything lined up for after this job?"

"I do." I grimaced and took another swig of my beer. "It pays good, but it'll be harder to conceal. There's a pig farmer two towns over who needs a few pens dug out and a small barn built. He's got the machinery for it. I'll have to figure out how to hide that smell."

"Change and wash your clothing at my house," Levi offered. "Just leave your boots outside."

"Thanks." I nodded. "Might be worth picking up a cheap pair I can toss afterward."

We fell into a collective silence after that. The good thing about being with people who knew everything about you and your life was that you didn't have to explain your decisions to them. They understood.

Levi had been one of the people in town my father had lent support to. Levi's father had left early on but had come back when Levi was in high school. Rather than sticking around and trying to make things work in Driverton, both of

Levi's parents had up and left. Without the help of my father and several other members of the community, Levi would have landed in government care. Instead, the town rallied and paid the mortgage on the house Levi lived in and made sure he was fed and clothed until he was old enough to pay those bills himself.

My father's dying wishes were as sacred to Levi as they were to me. And Katie? Even though she lived one town over, she'd practically grown up at my house. My mother was a second one to her and she'd hero-worshipped my father. She'd taken his death as hard as I had, and I hadn't handled it well.

I didn't realize what a stabilizing factor my father was, not only in my life but in Driverton, until he was gone. I was left adrift without a clue how to fill his shoes, but his loss was felt throughout the town. Quickly, after his death, a general sense of uncertainty began to pervade common discourse. People had become used to having a place to meet and build connections. They worried I'd sell, and how much Driverton would change if its casual meeting place closed. Only when I called for a town meeting and shared my plan to take over Little Willie's and continue to run it as my father had did things go back to normal.

How close I came to not being able to keep it open after taking it over was painfully obvious. A few weeks in I couldn't order enough food to continue feeding everyone. It was so damn humiliating when news of that spread and someone brought a meal to donate to the restaurant rather than ordering from the menu. I couldn't have felt like a bigger failure. I'm not proud of how I acted that day, how I refused it, walked out, and went to my father's grave, where I sat and cried.

Pete Glenford, a good friend of my father, had found me there. He didn't mention the tears I'd hastily wiped from my cheeks. He didn't mention how I'd embarrassed not only myself but the family who'd tried to donate the food. Instead, he stood beside me in quiet support until I got my emotions under control.

Eventually, he said something that I accepted like a drowning person being offered a raft. "Never needing help isn't a testament to a man's strength. Knowing when and how to accept it is. Your father knew how to help people without making them feel like he was giving them charity. Allowing people to pay it forward to you in appreciation of what he gave to them . . . that's not accepting charity . . . that's you giving them an opportunity to hold their heads high again."

In that moment, I felt that I was speaking to my father and for that reason alone, I shared the two things he'd asked of me. "I don't know if I can do it," I admitted. "There's so much debt and Little Willie's has cost more than it makes for a long time. I can't increase prices since some already eat there for free. I can't bring in other patrons without changing the nature of the place. I was saving up to go to school, that money is already gone. I can't give up, but I also don't see how I can do this."

"Son," Pete said, laying a hand on my shoulder, "you're not alone. If I could help you financially, I would, but what I *can* do is help you find ways to make money outside of Driverton. You won't lose Little Willie's and we'll keep your father's secrets. But you have an apology to deliver first."

Pete had been right about a lot of things. People were eager to help keep Little Willie's open, even if that meant sometimes bussing their own tables or bringing enough food to share with another family. And it did restore a light in many people's eyes.

Not necessarily my mother's. She was pretty sure I was mismanaging the restaurant since, in her eyes, it had never struggled in the past. She also had a lot to say about how little I did around the house after taking over Little Willie's. I didn't tell her about the extra jobs I worked during the hours I went missing from the restaurant. All she saw was how often I came home drunk and how much trouble Levi and I got into when we went anywhere together.

I took a bite of the sandwich and my eyes rounded. "*Megan* made this?"

Katie nodded. "With your mom's help. They said it's a combination of both of their secret ingredients."

Savoring a second bite, I fell a little in love . . . at least my stomach did. This time I did look around and was disappointed when I didn't see Megan.

Fully aware of what had my attention, Katie said, "She drove your mother home, but she said she'd be back. So, if you wait around . . ."

I took another bite in place of answering her. Sure, Megan was attractive and knew her way around the kitchen and smelled—I inhaled deeply as I remembered her scent—heavenly. But I had neither the time nor the energy for a woman who wanted more than a good time. Someone like Megan would never settle for what I'd offered others.

Honestly, I was working so much that lately a good nap often sounded more tempting than sex. *Not this morning though. No, Megan had me feeling alive in a way I hadn't in a long time.*

The level of how pathetic that thought was had me smiling with twisted humor as I finished my beer. *My life sucks.*

"You should steer clear of Megan, Ollie," Levi said.

Katie countered, "Not too easy when she's staying in the same house."

Levi met my gaze. "Doesn't matter. Everette looks serious about Shelby. We don't want to fuck with that."

"You say that like I'm the one who screws every woman I meet." It was low, but not so low that he didn't smile. We'd been friends for too long to not throw a good dig now and then.

"Maybe if you stayed sober a little more, you'd be good enough in the sack that you wouldn't find the pickings so slim."

Had the sandwich not been delicious, I would have

thrown it at him. "I'd refute that, but I don't remember everything I did last night."

"I heard you went down on her then fell asleep before you got yours," Levi said with a chuckle. "I mean, at least she got hers."

Katie put her fingers in her ears. "La la la, I don't need to hear this."

"No wonder I woke up with a boner."

Rising to her feet, Katie said, "I know that one day both of you will grow up. I pray it's soon."

"Katie," I said slowly.

She looked down at me, completely taken in by my conciliatory tone. "Yes?"

"Get us another round when you have a chance."

Huffing, she wagged a finger at the two of us. "I should say no."

I smirked and waved my empty mug at her. "Please?"

Hands on hips, she said, "Fine, but only because I work here. The two of you deserve to get your own damn beer."

"Hey," Levi said with a laugh. "How did I get in trouble?"

Katie pivoted to face him. "Do you even remember the name of who you were with last night?"

"Sure," Levi said without missing a beat. "Beautiful. I think that's what I called her."

"Disgusting," Katie said as she turned and walked away.

Both Levi and I burst out laughing. Her back straightened more, and she flounced away. "I'd give her a raise if I could afford to," I said.

"She deserves it for putting up with us," Levi agreed.

"She sure does." I turned my attention back to my meal. "One more beer and I should head out. There're a few things I need to pick up at the hardware store before I return to the Baxter's place."

"You want help tonight?"

"No, I've got it, thanks. You did more than enough today."

"I'm not helping you at that pig farm."

"Fair enough."

We ate in comfortable silence for a few, then Levi said, "Everette sure does look happy."

"He does."

"He asked me what happened the one day we trained with Bradford."

"What'd you say?"

"I told him it wasn't our scene. He was disappointed..."

I chewed a French fry before answering. "How Everette could put up with Bradford is a mystery to me. There's something wrong with that guy. I get his anger issues but killing as many people as he has... that changes a person. I don't trust him."

Levi shrugged. "Cooper does. So does Tom. They say there's no one better when it comes to bringing hostages home alive."

My eyes narrowed. "Why are you talking him up? You considering training with him again?"

Levi sighed. "Katie is. At least, I think so. She's not looking happy lately, Ollie."

"She quit too. No one forced her to."

"I know."

With impatience rising, I lowered my voice. "I don't have the luxury of being able to tell people to cover for me while I step outside of my life for a few months. You were there, Levi. You heard Bradford say training with him would be full-time, hard, manual labor until we have nothing left to give. I'm already at that point. He doesn't have to break me to build me up; I'm already a fucking disaster."

"I have some money set aside—"

"I'm okay, Levi. Thanks. Ignore the crap coming out of my mouth today, I didn't get enough sleep last night."

"That's not what she said," he quipped.

"Asshole." I barked out a laugh. "You do deserve to get your own beer."

Chapter Eight

Megan

AFTER COOKING, SHELBY had offered to let me spend the day with Everette and her, but it was clear they had things to talk out. I was close if she needed me and would be for at least another day. I only had a few days off from my job. I preferred to spend that time exploring Driverton and the surrounding area over acting as an unnecessary third wheel.

Together, Mrs. Williams and I delivered several trays of food to Little Willie's. I'd heard a lot about her family's restaurant but had pictured it poorly. From the outside, it didn't look like much. The hours on the sign near the entrance were faded to an unreadable level. I expected to walk in through the kitchen, but we parked next to the main entrance, and each carried one tray inside that way. As soon as we entered, several people who'd been seated at tables rushed toward us to ask if there was anything else in the car that needed to be brought in.

What struck me about the inside of the restaurant, beyond the rustic furnishings and wood—everything—was how clean and cheerful it was. The red and white checkered tablecloths that adorned each table looked freshly laundered. The small crowd of people eating were both young and old, and the chatter between tables made it feel more like a family gathering than a public space.

I liked it instantly.

This was the place Mrs. Williams's husband had envisioned then made a reality. It was a living testament to the good her husband had done and was so beautiful my eyes filled with tears. That was when Mrs. Williams told me to call her Reana. I'd like to think that was the moment we became friends.

I didn't hesitate, an hour later, as I walked back into Little Willie's alone. Everyone Reana had introduced me to had been welcoming. Katie, the only waitress Little Willie's employed, met me as soon as I stepped into the main area.

"Everyone loves your pulled pork," she announced with a huge smile. She was about my age but with an air of innocence that made me feel older.

"I can't take full credit for it. Reana taught me a few new tricks I'm definitely taking home with me."

"*Reana*," Katie parroted. "Everyone calls her Mrs. Williams."

I maintained my smile. "I can call her whatever you'd like me to."

"Did she say you could use her first name?"

I tipped my head to the side. "Is that a problem?"

"No. No. I'm just . . ." Katie stopped, seemed to reconsider what she'd almost said, then smiled again. "It's the opposite of being a problem. Come on in. Are you hungry?"

Walking beside her, I confessed. "Not really, just wanted to get out and see Driverton. I have no plans, though, if there's anything here you need help with. I don't mind washing dishes or clearing tables."

Katie looked me over. "Dressed like that?"

I let out a laugh/sigh. "I packed poorly for this trip, but I promise to do better when I come back. That said, this dress survived a morning of cooking. All I'd require is an apron and for you to point me to what you need done."

"You're serious?"

When it came to breaking the ice with a new crowd, there was no better way than to offer to help out. "Absolutely."

She waved for me to follow her, and for the second time that day, I donned an apron over a dress that had only ever seen social events before this trip. "You're technically company, and I've got nearly everyone used to washing their own dishes, but if you don't mind helping me deliver food to the tables, I'd appreciate the extra set of hands."

"Sure."

I trailed after Katie to an unattended bar. She walked behind it, filled two mugs of beer and handed them to me.

"Do you remember Levi and Ollie?"

My face flushed as I remembered Ollie a little too well. "Yes."

She nodded toward a corner of the room. "Would you mind taking these to them?"

"No problem," I said, swallowing hard, then walked across the room to where Levi and Ollie were seated.

They rose to their feet when I stopped at their table in what felt like an old-fashioned response to a woman appearing. I placed the beers on the table with the confidence I'd earned from years of waitressing in college.

"What are you doing?" Ollie demanded. His irritation surprised me.

"Helping?"

"Katie," his voice boomed across the room.

She waved to him and walked away. Her complete disregard for his command brought a smile to my lips. *Okay, so there's no bite behind his growl.*

Levi nodded toward an empty chair. "Would you like to join us?"

I shook my head.

He retook his seat. Ollie glared at where Katie had stood then at me. "She's pushing it lately."

My response was to hold his gaze and keep smiling. *Scowl away. All I see is an apple that didn't fall far from its tree.*

The air thickened unexpectedly, and for a moment, the rest of the world fell away. God, he had the kind of eyes a woman could lose herself in. "I asked if there was anything I could do. I don't mind."

"I do," he growled.

The smell of beer on his breath should have been a turn off. A lot of what I'd heard about him should have been, but when I looked into his eyes, I didn't see an irresponsible man who partied too much. There was a strength to him—a determination and yearning that touched my heart. Who was behind his gatekeeper personality? I would have bet my life he wasn't lazy or weak. I sensed frustration, disappointment, and . . . fatigue?

A quick glance down at his hands revealed something odd. Reana had shared her concerns that her son was drinking rather than facing his responsibilities, but his hands told another story. If he wasn't hardworking, why were they so calloused? How was someone who slept in, slept out, and drank too much also muscular?

"Too bad," I said softly.

His eyebrows shot up. "What did you say?"

"The apron is already on." I met his gaze in challenge. "So, unless you intend to take it off me, I'd sit your ass down and drink your beer."

Levi guffawed then coughed.

Ollie's nostrils flared, and the air sizzled. It was easy to imagine him tossing me over his shoulder and carrying me off to the bed of his truck. I was a modern woman who would have previously said I liked my men a little more sophisticated, but damn he was hot.

"Sit," Levi said forcefully.

Desire and something else raged in Ollie's eyes before he swore under his breath. "Don't mind me," he said a bit petulantly. "I only own the place."

My small win didn't feel like one. I could have walked away with my head held high, but I hated the tired slump of his shoulders. "I didn't know what to think of this town when Shelby told me about it, but I'm glad I get to experience it firsthand. It might seem silly, but working here, even if it's only for a day, is an honor for me. I love everything about the reason your father opened the place and that you're continuing his legacy. Everything about it is beautiful."

I'd expected my words to bring him comfort, but instead they seemed to annoy him. "Work here all you want, but no one's paying you for it."

"Oh, of course not—"

"And you can kiss up to my mother, but you won't be staying at our house again."

"Ouch," I said. That one was unexpected and stung. "I would never expect to."

"Ollie, shut up," Levi said.

"And to be clear, I don't care how good of a cook you are, you're not my type."

That one gave me pause, then brought a smile to my face. "What?"

In a low tone, Levi warned, "Don't do it."

Ollie inhaled deeply, then plowed on, "Listen, if things work out between Shelby and Everette, we'll probably see more of you. I don't want either of us to get confused." A flush reddened his neck.

"Because I can *cook?*" I asked, becoming more and more amused the more uncomfortable he looked. I laughed. "I've heard the old saying about the way to a man's heart is through his stomach, but I had no idea there was any truth to it. Did my pulled pork give you the feelies for me?"

He neither confirmed nor denied that. The corner of his mouth twitched, and I was glad I'd never been one to retreat. He'd made two things clear. One, he was attracted to me. Two, he didn't want to be. He was right that we'd likely be part of each other's lives if Shelby and Everette ended up together, so we did need to figure out how to get along.

When he simply held my gaze with an indiscernible expression, I winked. "If I promise to cook less, can we be friends?"

His eyes narrowed and he sank to his seat.

I stood there, telling myself I should go, but I couldn't help myself. I laid a hand on one of his strong shoulders, bent, and said, "I'm sorry, I have a sarcastic sense of humor."

Ollie's expression softened. "And here I thought you were sweet, but it looks like Turtle Lady has layers."

Another spark of interest jolted through me. I retracted my hand. "Just like you."

He searched my face and time suspended again. An onlooker might have thought his declaration that I wasn't his type came out of nowhere, but something was bubbling between us. He knew that I knew it. I could joke and try to diffuse it, but something in him was pulling at something in me. We felt—*inevitable*.

Sadness filled his eyes. "I'm not whoever it is you think you see in me."

Whatever I would have answered was left unsaid when Katie appeared at my side. "I finally have some help, could you not monopolize her?"

Reluctantly I tore my gaze from Ollie's and smiled at Katie. "What do you need?"

I didn't hear what she said as she led me away. My attention was on the conversation happening behind us.

Levi said, "What the hell is wrong with you?"

I would have paid a year of my salary to have stayed within hearing distance of Ollie's answer, but sadly Katie's voice drowned it out. She led me through the kitchen and right out the back door. Only when the door closed behind us did she say, "I probably shouldn't say anything . . ."

Not too much good ever followed those words. "Am I fired?" I joked.

Her expression was instantly apologetic. "Oh my God, no. This isn't about you. It's about Ollie. There's obviously a spark between the two of you."

I waited rather than giving anything away.

She continued, "I love my cousin. He has a big heart and

would give anyone in need the shirt off his back . . ."

The mistake many people made was assuming they knew what the other person was thinking. It was better to give a person time to speak their mind rather than getting preemptively defensive. So, I kept my expression approachable, and my mouth shut.

Katie chewed her lip, glanced at the closed door behind us, and said, "He has more on his plate than he'll ever admit to and that often makes him grumpy. You seem not only nice but like someone who has her life together. Please don't lead him on."

I frowned. "Why would you think I'd do that?"

"That came out wrong. What I'm trying to say is that you seem amazing."

"And *he's not?*" I didn't like the idea that Ollie's cousin saw him that way and it brought out a protective side of me.

She waved a hand. "Ollie's loyal, hardworking, generous . . ."

"Sounds like a real asshole."

"But he's struggling and won't accept help. I know how hard he's trying to keep everything together and his head above water. I just don't want to see him get his heart broken because you came into his life before he was ready for someone like you."

That was a lot to process. "You're afraid *he'll* get hurt?"

She nodded.

I tucked my hands into the front pockets of the apron.

"I'm no femme fatale."

"I'm sorry, I don't speak French."

Okay. I hooked my head to the side and kept a straight face. "What I meant was I'm not the kind of woman who has to fend men off. I'm sure he'll be fine."

She let out an audible breath. "I know my cousin and he doesn't look at anyone the way he was looking at you." She brushed a loose lock of hair out of her eyes. "There's a lot I can't say, but things are changing in Driverton and there are opportunities being presented to all of us that I'm hoping Ollie will take advantage of. A year from now he might be someone you—"

"Wow," I burst out. "I hope no one I love thinks as little of me as you think of him."

All friendliness left her expression. "All I'm doing is looking out for him."

The rawness of her voice made me think she believed that. "Then maybe have a little faith in him."

"I have a lot of faith in him, but I also know him well enough to know—"

"That he doesn't deserve to have someone care about him?" I probably shouldn't have said that aloud, but her definition of having faith in someone didn't match mine.

"We all care about him." Her lips pressed together in an unhappy line. "I love my cousin."

"I never said you didn't."

"The more we talk the more my opinion of you is changing."

"That's probably a good thing because I don't agree with you, and I'm not someone who will pretend to."

"You fuck with Ollie, and I'll come for you."

I put both hands up in surrender. We obviously didn't communicate the same way. "I'm only here for a couple days. I have a job and a whole life out there. You've got nothing to worry about."

Some of the anger left her. "That's exactly why I'm worried. Ollie would be one of many good things in your life, but he'd see you as the only good in his. You could break his heart, then Levi would have to help me bury your body and he hates digging graves."

I laughed at her joke.

At least, I hoped it was a joke.

I took off the apron and handed it back to Katie. "I think it's best if I explore somewhere else in Driverton."

"I agree," Katie said as she accepted the apron.

I wasn't used to people not liking me, but I didn't think my usual approach would sway Katie. She saw me as a threat to her cousin. No amount of smiling would change that. Time would, though.

I drove back to Ollie's house and had tea with Reana. When she asked me how things had gone at Little Willie's I didn't mention anything negative. I told her how nice everyone was and the compliment we'd received about our pulled pork.

I didn't ask if there were any missing outsiders or fresh graves in Driverton. I was sure I didn't want to know.

Chapter Nine

>>><<<

Ollie

IT WAS LATE when I dragged myself up the stairs that led to my bedroom. My mother's room was on the first floor. I had the privilege of sharing the second floor with any and all guests she invited to stay with us. The door of one bedroom was open and seemed empty—Shelby's. The next door was closed, but the light was on.

I should have walked past it. I was exhausted by the time I'd finished at the Baxter's—too tired to even drink—now, that's tired. I paused, though, and thought about how ungrateful I must have seemed to Megan.

Almost of its own accord, my hand met the wood of the door and knocked softly. When there wasn't an immediate response, I told myself to walk away, but I stayed there.

A moment later, the door opened, and Megan's eyes widened. "Oh, it's you. I thought it was Shelby."

After a quick glance down at the delicious expanse of legs her mid-thigh nightshirt revealed, I glued my gaze to her face. It was a struggle to remember what had felt imperative to say a moment earlier. My voice was gruff when I finally spoke. "Thank you for cooking today and for delivering it."

"You're welcome."

"And for offering to help out at the restaurant. I didn't mean to be a dick about that."

"I understand. My cooking is so good it got you all kinds of confused. It happens."

I coughed on a laugh. "I'm sure it does."

The way she looked up at me—hell, the way I felt when I saw myself in her eyes—I can't explain it, but it made me feel both good and bad at the same time. "Katie said she had a few words with you but wouldn't tell me what it was about."

"It was nothing."

"It was enough that you didn't come back in."

She shrugged and I did my damnedest not to notice how that made her hardening nipples dance beneath her shirt.

I cleared my throat. "Driverton doesn't get a lot of outside traffic. If she said anything that offended you, it was likely due to that. She's all heart. Give her another chance and she'll probably adore you by tomorrow."

"It might take more than a day, but I'm okay with that. It takes me a bit to trust new people as well."

"That's kind of you."

"Not really. Just true. I think of people like morning glories. If you're patient sometimes they'll unfold into something beautiful."

That wasn't at all how I saw people, but arguing was the last thing on my mind. The sheer act of keeping my thoughts off all the things I wanted to do to her was making it difficult to think of much else. "Well, I didn't want you to go to sleep thinking I wasn't grateful for your help today."

She studied my face and brought one hand to cup a side of it. "I don't know what weight you're carrying, but you have a lot of people in your life who care about you. I hope you let them."

I blinked back a wave of confusing emotions that were quickly followed by anger. "I don't know what Katie told you, but—"

Megan lowered her hand. "I'm not from here so you don't have to lie to me. You don't smell like a bar. You smell like paint and construction dust. Go get some rest and stop worrying about what a stranger thinks about anything."

"I don't care what anyone thinks about me." That was a lie. I knew it. She knew it. But I felt compelled to say it.

"Okay."

"Goodnight."

"Goodnight."

Still, I remained.

She leaned toward me.

I leaned toward her.

The brush of her lips against mine sent shockwaves through me and I straightened.

After she shut the door, I gasped for air and forced myself to walk down the hall to my room. Once inside, I sagged backward against the wall and slammed it with a fisted hand.

Chapter Ten

Megan

LEANING AGAINST THE inside of my door, I brought a shaking hand to my lips. *I kissed him. Or he kissed me.* It happened so fast I couldn't say which of us had initiated or ended it. All I knew was that no kiss had ever rocketed through me as that one had.

Not my first when I'd still been in braces and hadn't yet sorted out the difference between a crush and love. My heart had thudded just as fast for that kiss, but for entirely different reasons. Back then the unknown had been more exciting than the actual event.

Not the one that had led to me losing my virginity years later with someone I'd thought would stay with me forever. Like kindling lit without fuel beneath it, we'd burned hot for a short time but it hadn't lasted. We'd been too young and immature to mean any of the promises we'd made each other. I wasn't angry when I looked back at our time together. Our breakup hadn't started or ended with a fight. Odd how that can happen.

I wasn't a woman men stopped in their tracks to take a second look at, but my social calendar contained dates on a regular basis—just not with anyone I felt I couldn't live without. They liked me. I liked them. We could have sex if I implied I was willing to, but I didn't do that often because I was holding out for someone I felt more for than only a physical attraction.

This thing with Ollie was hitting me hard. I wanted to go downstairs, wake his mother, and tell her to take a second and kinder look at her son. I wanted to track down his cousin and ask her why she wasn't stepping up more for him if she knew he was struggling.

I was also fighting an irrational urge to sprint down the hallway to Ollie's room, slip inside, snuggle into his arms, and . . . that's what didn't make sense. We weren't friends. I couldn't see a feasible way we could date even if he asked me out.

So, what was it I wanted from him? Sex? I could find that easily back home and with less potential complication. Did I think I could save him? Was that who I was now? One of those delusional women who saw a damaged man and volunteered themselves as tribute?

I froze as another light knock vibrated against my back. If it was Ollie, I shouldn't open the door. Or should I? Would he be someone I regretted being with or the one who made me forever wonder what could have been?

Taking a deep breath, I opened the door.

Shelby swept past me with a grateful smile. She was with the dog Everette had given her. After telling the dog to sit, she plopped on the corner of my bed. "I'm so glad you're up. You need to tell me if I'm losing my sanity."

I closed my door slowly and told myself I was relieved it hadn't been Ollie. "You're not losing your mind." I bent to greet Tyr but spoke to Shelby in a tone that made the dog feel like I was praising him. "It's impossible to lose something you never had."

She laughed. "Thanks for the reality check, friend."

"Anytime." I straightened and lay on the bed beside her, my legs dangling off the end beside hers. Tyr jumped onto the bed and chose the spot right above our heads to lie down. "I'm ready—spill."

After a moment, she said quietly. "I want to stay here and give this a real chance. I don't know what that means as far as what I'll do for a living or how long Mrs. Williams will be okay with me staying here. I never saw myself as someone who'd enjoy a small town . . ."

"What are you worried about, Shelby?"

"I've done a lot of running and hiding since losing my parents. I don't feel like that's what I'm doing this time, but how can I be sure?"

Her question mirrored the ones I was asking myself so I took a few minutes to find an answer within me. "I don't think you can know without giving yourself time to experience it. From the outside, I see only good changes in you. Everette has brought a sparkle back to your eyes and it seems like the healthy lifestyle he's embracing is just what you need, but only you know if that's enough."

"I'm scared, Megan. What if I rebuild my life around Everette and he doesn't do the same with me?" She expelled a shaky breath. "What if I lose him too?"

She was hitting these impossibly tough questions out of the park. I didn't know what to say . . . until I did. "We're not promised anything in life. He could devote his entire life to you then die in a car accident tomorrow."

"I'm painfully aware of that."

"The only way to avoid that kind of potential loss is to never care about anyone again. Not a man. Not me. Because I have no intention of going anywhere, but I also have no control over when my ticket is called."

"This is making me feel worse."

I rolled onto my side so I was facing her profile. "I could lie and tell you that if you stay here your life will be perfect and nothing bad will ever happen to you again, but we've both seen too much to believe that. Everette seems like a good man who cares for you deeply. And from what I can tell, you care for him just as much. If that's not enough to make something worth gambling on, I don't know what is."

She rolled to face me. "How do you always know what to say to make me feel better?"

"The way you always know what I need to hear."

We shared the smile friends do when they've been through hell and back and come out the other side still together and stronger. After a moment, she asked, "What did you end up doing today?"

"I dropped off the food with Reana then explored the town a little. It's an interesting place."

"In what way?"

"We both grew up in a town where people moved in and out regularly. In my current apartment building I know the names of maybe two people. We all just nod and smile when we pass each other in the hallways. In Driverton everyone seems to know everyone and some families have been here for generations."

"Do you think it'll be difficult for them to accept an outsider?"

Other than Katie's response to me, I'd only been welcomed. "I don't think so. People do move here. I met more than one newbie today. The man Everette works with, Bradford, he and his wife bought a place on the edge of town. They run a mini-horse rescue and are looking to open a second. The others seem equally friendly. I stopped to check out a fresh produce stand at one house and they invited me in for some pie. The Kirby family. Normally I'd run in the other direction from an offer from strangers, but I was curious. I met Mama Kirby, Grandma Kirby, Grandpa Kirby, their neighbor, and it was really nice. Their coffee was top tier, but I'd misunderstood the pie part. Do you know what a whoopie pie is?"

"Maybe? Isn't that two chocolate cookies with cream in the middle? They sell them in supermarkets?"

"Something like that. These are homemade and they come in all different flavors. The cookies are really cake and the filling—let's just say I'm going home heavier than I came here. They were that good."

"I'll have to check them out."

"Yes, you will. In fact I promised the grandmother if you learned how to make them, you'd teach me and we'd all enter the annual Dover Whoopie Pie Festival Best Flavor contest next year. The family I met used to win it every year until their children moved away and they no longer felt it was worth the trip out there. I promised them if we were still around we'd take them."

Shelby blinked a few times quickly. "Next year. I'm trying to wrap my head around next week."

I sat up. "If you're not here, you're not here. But if you are, how cool would that be? And you'd have made some new friends."

She pushed herself into a seated position as well. "You're always better at meeting people than I am."

"It's not a skill as much as it's a decision. I make myself okay with putting myself out there. If you sit inside waiting for the world to come to you, you'll sit alone for a very long time. I'd rather meet ten people and like two of them than meet no one."

"Okay, okay, message received. I spent today mostly with Everette, but I'll widen my circle."

"Good." I glanced at my luggage. "I can stay for one more night but then I need to head back."

"Would you like me to ask Clay if you can fly out in the same style we arrived in?"

"Duh," I said with a laugh. "No need for it to be staffed though. Actually, it'll be better for me if it's not. I'll just bring a book to read."

"Sounds like a good plan." She leaned over and hugged me. "Thank you again for coming here with me."

"Stop." I said with a laugh. "You'd do it for me."

"I would." She stood and looked down at me with concern. "Would you like to spend the day with Everette and me?"

I swung my feet back and forth. "Nah. You'd only slow my adventures down. I've got people to meet and whoopie pies to taste."

She stretched and yawned. "If you change your mind . . ."

"I won't. But I will see you at breakfast."

She called Tyr to her side and gave me one last hug before leaving my bedroom and closing the door behind her. I was about to lie down and go to sleep but decided I should use the bathroom one more time before I did.

With the advice I'd given Shelby still sloshing around in my thoughts, I dug a notepad out of my purse and wrote my number on it along with a quick note:

I have one final day to explore Driverton before I go home. If you'd like to give me tips on where to go or to show me around, text me.

Megan

I read the note over. It was a bold move, but anything worth having in life was worth reaching for. I didn't know what I wanted from Ollie, but I knew I wanted to see him again before I left. If he didn't feel the same, well, at least I'd followed my heart.

His room was at the end of the hall. I walked to the door of it, bent down, stuffed the note beneath his door, and scurried to the bathroom. I half expected to see him standing in the hall when I stepped out again, but he wasn't.

Back in my room, I kept the phone near me as I tucked myself in for the night. I checked for a message from him before and after I'd turned off the lights. Disappointment settled in the more time passed and embarrassment circled.

There was a chance he was already sleeping and hadn't seen the note.

There was an equal chance he saw it being delivered and decided that since he was no longer in grade school, he wasn't interested in secretly passing notes.

I groaned. I should have just knocked on his door like he'd knocked on mine and asked him if he'd like to hang out with me the next day. That would have been a thousand times more mature.

Sleep was difficult to achieve, but I finally did. I woke the next morning feeling anything but refreshed. After throwing the covers back, I checked the time on my phone and was happy I hadn't slept in and missed breakfast. It was then that I saw I had a message from an unknown number.

All it said was: **Okay**

Okay, what? Okay, he'd give me tips for where to visit? Okay, he'd show me around?

I checked the time on the message—about a half hour earlier. When I opened the door of my room, I heard the sound of the shower and looked up and down the hallway in an attempt to determine who was using it.

On impulse, I tested something. I sent Ollie a message. **What time?** Either he'd give me one or explain that I'd misunderstood.

A phone beeped inside the bathroom and I froze. The water turned off. Heat flooded me as I imagined him standing there, naked and dripping wet, reading my text.

Right after breakfast

I bit my lip and closed my eyes as I remembered how good his mouth had felt on mine. I fought back the desire to throw open the bathroom door and taste him again. Drawn to him. Craving him. How was it possible to feel that way about someone I hardly knew?

Did such a strong reaction mean it was real?

Or was it a primal attraction that would lead nowhere good?

I typed: **Okay**, then deleted it.
See you downstairs.
I deleted that as well.

I brought the phone up near my face, reread our brief messages to each other and told myself he probably wasn't expecting a response from me. I should leave it like that and head down to breakfast. Except, shit I was still in my nightshirt. Right. I should get dressed then go down to breakfast. After I shower, which I can't do yet because . . .

"Who are you texting?" Ollie asked in an amused voice.

His bare feet came into view first as I went from looking at my phone, to wishing I could disappear into the floor, to wondering if he could possibly be as good looking as I remembered him. Slowly, I took in his jean-clad lower half. Long legs, muscular thighs, big . . . nope, I would not get caught looking there twice.

My eyes followed his zipper up to the edge of his jeans where they hung low exposing the full length of his flat abs. Although he didn't have the bulging muscles of men who spent their lives in gyms, it was obvious that Ollie was no stranger to manual labor. I was tempted to run my hands over his toned pecs. When I finally did raise my eyes to meet his, he was smiling and I couldn't remember what he'd asked. "I'm sorry?"

The heat in his gaze told me I wasn't the only one affected by our proximity. "It's dangerous to keep meeting like this. You get better looking every time I see you."

My hand flew up to what had to be wild bed hair. "You

do too," I said in a strangled voice.

He smiled. I melted and wondered why I'd ever wasted my time with men who made me feel less alive than this.

With an apologetic tilt of his head, he said, "I don't have a lot of time today, but I can give you a tour this morning. The town's not that big."

"Working at the restaurant today?"

"Part of the day. I have some things to do."

There was something in his eyes when he evaded my question that pulled at my heart. Where did he go when he wasn't at Little Willie's? What was he hiding? "I could help." As soon as I said the words I wished I could retract them.

"Thanks, but it's not something you'd enjoy."

"You don't know that."

"This is a bad idea." He swung the towel he'd been holding up around his neck. "Don't go on the tour with me. Go back to wherever you came from and whoever you're dating back there."

"First"—my chin rose as I spoke—"don't tell me what to do. Second, if they were important to me, they'd be here."

"They?" he straightened and frowned. "How many men are you dating?"

"Before I share that kind of information, you have to get to know me."

He closed the distance between us and backed me till I was against the wall. With one hand on the wall beside my head, he leaned closer. "I'll play any game you want to, but don't expect it to lead anywhere. If you're okay with that, I'm in."

The intensity of his gaze temporarily had my heart racing, but then an intrusive thought brought a smile to my lips. "Do women actually accept that line?"

"All the time."

"Wow, you may need to expand your social circle."

One side of his mouth curled. "As a woman with her own entourage of male company, tell me, what works with you?"

I ignored the little dig and answered. "Respect. Honesty. Friendship."

He leaned in closer, so close I could feel the heat of his breath on my lips. "So, they know about each other?"

I cleared my throat. "When all you're doing is meeting for dinner and a movie you don't have to disclose the details of what you do the rest of the week."

"How many?"

"I told you, none of them are serious."

"How many men take you to dinner on a regular basis?"

"Some are just friends."

He cupped my jaw and brought my face up so my eyes met his. "I don't like this."

"What?" I whispered.

He ran a thumb over my lower lip. "Caring if you're bullshitting me or not."

It was difficult to breathe while looking into his eyes, but I did my best to sound unflustered. "Take me on a tour and show me what you think I can't be trusted knowing, and I'll tell you whatever you want to know."

He bent his head and lightly brushed his lips over mine. The connection was so brief I nearly cried when it ended abruptly. "I bet I could get you to tell me anyway."

I gave in to the temptation and ran my hands up his stomach to caress his chest. "I bet you don't know me well enough to know what you could or couldn't get me to do."

Desire flared in his eyes and every inch of me was on fire for him. "All of this is a bad idea."

"Maybe." I couldn't disagree. "But I want to know where you go when you leave Little Willie's."

"Why do you care?"

I shrugged. "I don't know, but I do."

He nodded. "Yeah, me too." He pushed himself back from me and the wall. "Did you pack anything other than a dress?"

"I have sleep shorts and a T-shirt."

"Bring them. You might need them."

"Okay."

"And get your ass in the shower before I risk getting evicted and join you."

Rather than seeing that as a bad thing, I fluttered my eyelashes at him and joked, "You'd do that for me?"

His laugh was a rumble in his chest before it burst out. "Turtle Lady, you scare the hell out of me."

I wrinkled my nose at him. "I'm not trying to."

"I know," he said in a gruff tone. "That's the scary part."

Chapter Eleven

Ollie

I BEAT MEGAN downstairs. My mother and Shelby were filling plates with food when I entered the kitchen.

"Look who's here bright and early," my mother said. "And showered."

I gave her a kiss on the cheek. "You say that like it's a rare thing."

"How would I know?" She stepped back. "I hardly see you lately. The only proof I have that you still live here is that food goes missing in the night."

There was no way to productively engage in that line of conversation, so I turned to Shelby instead. "What do you think of Driverton so far?"

Her smile was so bright it seemed a little forced. "It's wonderful. Everyone is wonderful."

I met her smile with sympathy. "It takes time to feel comfortable in a new place."

"Yes," she agreed emphatically. "Did you see Megan upstairs? Is she up? Everette will be here soon."

"I heard the shower going." That was true at least. "So I imagine she won't be too much longer."

"Oh, good." Shelby poured herself a cup of coffee. "She leaves tomorrow. I feel so bad about not spending more time with her. I hope she gets out and does something."

"I offered to show her around." I regretted voicing that aloud as soon as I saw my mother's expression go from mildly interested to fully invested.

"You did?" my mother asked. "Where are you taking her?"

"I'll figure something out," I said evasively. It would have been better to say nothing to my mother.

"I don't want to hear that you took her drinking," she said. *Yep, I should have kept my mouth shut.*

"Wasn't intending to."

"And stay away from Mr. Arnold's plums." She looked over at Shelby. "One day they're going to get that man arrested. He doesn't like people on his property without permission and will shoot his salt shotgun at anyone who trespasses. The worst thing we ever did was tell the kids to stay away because of that. The damn fools took it like a dare and now it's practically a rite of passage for young kids in this town. He's a nice enough man to give a bushel of plums if you ask, but no, this generation has to test him."

I poured myself a cup of coffee. "Mom, I'm not a kid anymore . . ."

Her hands went to her hips. "Did you or did you not take Bradford there when he first came to town?"

I sipped the piping hot coffee and mumbled, "It wasn't just me and none of us got hurt. Bradford was actually impressed with our stealth skills."

She shook her head and spoke to Shelby again. "I know you hold Bradford in high regard, but leave him with my son, Levi, Everette, and moonshine and they're . . . unpredictable."

Shelby paused and met my gaze. "Everette credits working with Bradford as the reason he's no longer drinking and why he's working on—"

"You don't have to explain one of my best friends to me," I snapped.

"Ollie," my mother said my name as a reprimand.

A quick look at Shelby's hurt expression confirmed I was in the wrong. "Sorry, Shelby. I'm happy for Everette and glad he found you. Don't listen to any of the shit that comes out of my mouth first thing in the morning."

After giving me a long look, her expression softened. "No, I'm sorry. I'm in your house and you don't know me. I completely understand why this conversation wouldn't be one you'd want to have with me here. So, how about some fruit? I just cut some up."

It was at that moment that I saw why Everette had fallen for this woman. "Thank you." I looked around. "What's left to do? I can scramble some eggs."

"I love eggs," she said, and we were back to being good.

My mother sighed. "I don't want you working with Bradford, Ollie, but I do think you should find something that you're passionate about—something you care about more than drinking."

It wasn't the first time she'd said that to me and it likely wouldn't be the last. My mother meant well and genuinely wanted the best for everyone around her. She could deliver a baby, clean and stitch wounds, and stop the most hardened man from swearing with just a look, but that didn't make it easier to be her son.

She loved me—but respect me? I often wondered.

I couldn't blame her. Everette, Levi, and I had run wild and stupid for more years than we should have. Back then drinking had been for fun and rebelling had made us feel invincible. Lately, all I felt was tired, and drinking brought only escape.

I didn't like that; despite being happy for Everette, a part of me resented I didn't have the ability to step outside my life and come back with not just a new skill but a whole new outlook—and what appeared to be a loving partner. Freedom felt so outside of my reach I had to tell myself I didn't want it.

Megan entered the kitchen, and her bright smile pushed every dark thought out of my head. Shelby's demeanor changed from tentative to happy. Even my mother, someone who was usually guarded around new people, lit up when she saw Megan.

"Sorry I'm late." Megan's voice was breathless.

"You're actually right on time," my mother said.

Shelby greeted her with a hug. "We were just talking about you."

"All good things, I hope," Megan answered sweetly before turning her attention to me. "Good morning."

Soft and feminine in a flowered version of the dress she'd worn the day before, she could have taken the hand of nearly any man in Driverton, single or married, and walked straight out of town with him. God, she was beautiful. "Morning."

Returning to the task of setting the table for breakfast, Shelby said, "Ollie was telling us that he's going to show you around today. That sounds like fun."

"I'm sure it will be." With all her attention on me, Megan said, "And I'm grateful for the opportunity."

Unused to anyone looking at me with that amount of optimism, I joked, "You may not be saying that after you see where I take you."

My mother's sound of disapproval in the background wasn't enough to tear my gaze from Megan. Megan didn't look away either. My breathing shallowed, and for a moment I wasn't struggling and losing a bit more of myself daily. I felt like anything and everything was possible—at least until she looked away.

An awkward silence followed.

"Making eggs?" she asked.

I held up a carton of them as well as a bowl and nodded because my stupid self couldn't think of a single thing to say.

She stepped closer and tilted her head upward toward me. "Would you like some help?"

I swallowed hard. "It's not very complicated."

"Yours are probably amazing, but my mother taught me a few tricks on how to make them fluffy and light. Would you like me to show you what she does?"

Thankfully, both my mother and Shelby moved away to the table. I squared my shoulders and held out the bowl to her. "Sure."

Now I can't say I paid much attention at all to her instructions, but I loved watching her expression change as she talked about her family. It was obvious she loved them but equally obvious their relationship was complicated. I could have stood there all day watching her delicately crack eggs and work a whisk through them. She had to ask me twice to turn a burner on to heat the pan she'd handed me.

When she held up a plate of eggs that looked almost exactly like every plate of eggs I'd ever seen, her face glowed with pride, and I would have taken down anyone who'd implied either she or her eggs weren't perfection. "They look amazing."

Her smile widened. "Thanks."

She turned away to carry the plate to the table and I slumped like someone had deflated me. Simply by being near me, she'd had me standing taller and prouder. It was scary to think anyone could have that effect on me.

I took my place at the table and let the women talk. My brain felt as scrambled as the eggs and I wasn't about to risk saying anything that would ruin my chance of spending time with Megan that day.

We'd finished eating and had cleaned up when Everette arrived. His family was looking forward to spending time with Shelby, so he spirited her away. Megan excused herself to get something out of her room.

I was standing by the sink, drying the last of the dishes, when my mother came to stand beside me. "Ollie."

"Yes?" I placed the dried plate in the cabinet with the rest.

"I didn't mean to embarrass you earlier."

I sucked in a breath, turned so I was leaning against the counter, and put my hands in the front pockets of my jeans. "I know."

"It's just that I worry about you."

Without meeting her gaze, I said, "There's no need to."

"I know I push you, but it's only because I want the best for you."

What could I say to that? It was true.

She continued, "If Little Willie's ever becomes too much for you—"

"That'll never happen," I growled.

"It was your father's dream, not yours. Maybe it's time—"

"Mom, stop." This time I looked her in the eye. "I love

you, but I don't want to have this conversation."

She sighed then pressed her lips together. After a moment, she said, "How about a hug? Can I have that much?"

"Always." I pushed off and gathered her small frame to mine.

There was a time when she'd been the one I turned to with all my secrets. Yes, she spoke in a stern tone, but she was always there to patch me up when I fell and build me up when I doubted myself. We'd lost more than my father when he'd died, and I didn't know how to get it back. So, I just held her until Megan returned with her backpack.

Megan's mouth rounded, and our eyes met over my mother's head. "I'm sorry. I didn't mean to interrupt."

My mother sniffed and stepped out of my arms. "You're not. Sometimes a mother just needs a hug."

A son too. But I didn't say that. Instead, I nodded toward Megan. "Ready?"

She held up her bag. "Adventure, here I come."

That brought a reluctant smile to my lips. "Now I'll have to think of somewhere good to take you."

She swung the backpack over her shoulders. "I don't actually care what I see as long as you make sure it somehow involves Whoopie pies."

"Whoopie pies?" my mother echoed in surprise.

Megan laughed. "I had some at the Kirby's yesterday and they were out of this world delicious. So good, I promised if Shelby's still here next year, we'll learn their recipe and take them to the Dover Whoopie Pie Festival and enter them."

My mother's eyes narrowed. "And what did the Kirbys say to that?"

"They loved the idea," Megan said enthusiastically. "They miss it but haven't been since their kids moved away."

"Their recipe has been passed down for generations and they don't share it with anyone," my mother said.

Megan shrugged. "I'll take them even if they don't teach me how to make them. It seemed to mean a lot to them."

My mother turned and looked me in the eye, and I could almost hear her tell me Megan was a keeper. I looked away because I was in no position to meet anyone of quality. I had nothing to offer Megan and, honestly, most days, I didn't like myself all that much. She could do a hell of a lot better with probably any of those guys she was dating.

I nodded for Megan to follow me, then held the outside door open for her to walk through first. "We'll take my truck," I said abruptly.

Walking over to the passenger side I opened the door for her. Despite her dress and small stature, she climbed in like a pro. Once belted in, she smoothed the skirt of her dress down then turned and caught me looking at her. "What?"

I lacked the words to articulate how I felt in that moment because I—*ached*... both for her and for everything she represented. "Watch your feet." My tone was unnecessarily harsh. She looked down to check if she was in any danger of getting hurt, then met my gaze in confusion. I slammed the door and cursed.

After climbing into the driver's seat, I started the engine immediately and threw the truck into reverse. I was in the process of telling myself I was being an idiot when she laid a hand on my thigh, and I nearly drove us into a ditch.

"Are you okay?" she asked.

I righted the truck and joked, "Mentally? No. Physically? Also no."

"You're funny." As if only then realizing her touch's intimacy, she removed her hand.

I groaned, told myself I had no business feeling anything for her, then reached for her hand anyway and brought it back to where it had rested just above my knee. "And you're dangerously addictive."

"Dangerously addictive?" She repeated the words with a huge smile. "No one has ever said that about me."

My hand tightened on hers. "Not even the ones who feed you weekly?"

Her laugh was light. "Nope. Not even them."

"I wonder how many broken hearts you've left in your wake."

"I wonder the same about you."

I coughed on that one. "That's easy, only the ones who made the mistake of falling for me."

She chuckled. "That's a good line. Mind if I steal it? It's cocky and dark. Kind of hot, actually. I'm not sure if I could pull it off."

"Are you mocking me?"

Her smile didn't waver. "A little. I'm not really the type to let people get away with wallowing. Shelby went through some tough times . . ."

"Everette told us."

"She needed to heal, but she also needed to be prodded now and then. Shit happens. Sometimes life sucks. We can't let it beat us."

Being as attracted to her as I was should have had me strutting and trying to impress her, but our connection felt too real for that. We weren't on a date. She'd wanted to see what I was hiding and for some inexplicable reason, I wanted to show her. "I was born in Driverton. I'll probably die here. I used to sound like you, but lately life is kicking my ass."

"Is that why you drink?"

There was no judgment in her question, so it didn't offend me. "It takes the edge off, you know?"

She nodded. "I don't, but I believe you."

We drove a while in silence, crossing the town line and leaving Driverton behind. I pulled up the long driveway that led to Baxter's home and parked on the side of a two-story addition. "I built that," I said.

"The house?"

"This part of it."

"It's beautiful."

"And not finished. I have most of the painting done. Today I'm doing touchups and trim. How are you at painting?"

I'm not sure what I expected from her, but she unclipped her seatbelt and spun toward me with eyes shining with happiness. "You're working side jobs when you're not at Little Willie's."

I nodded.

She clasped her hands. "I knew it."

The pride in her eyes had my emotions jumbling. "It's not always this impressive. My next job is a pig farm cleanup and barn build. That one will be harder to conceal."

I wasn't sure what to think of the tears that shone in her eyes. "Why? Why the secrecy?"

I shrugged.

She wiped the corner of one of her eyes. "Katie knows what you do."

I nodded.

She sniffed. "Levi too."

"Couldn't have done this job without him."

"But not your mother?"

"She can't know."

Her hand flew to her mouth and tears filled her eyes again. "There's no way Little Willie's can be profitable—not with as much as you give away. That's what you're doing, isn't it? You're working on the side to afford to keep it open."

"Yes."

"Your father's legacy."

I shrugged and looked away. I wasn't eager to talk about the promises I'd made my father or how I wasn't exactly excelling at keeping them.

Her voice was so soft I had to strain to hear her. "You're a good person, Ollie Williams. I knew it the first time I looked into your eyes."

"We all see what we want to see when we're drunk." I inhaled. "What are you doing here with me? You deserve—"

"If that's the pity-party train pulling in, I didn't buy a ticket for that ride."

My attention snapped back to her. "What did you say?"

She looked me right in the eye. "You heard me. I'm here to learn more about you and to help you paint if you'd like the help. If you want me to agree that you're an awful person, I'd rather go find some Whoopie pies. You're the person you wake up and decide to be each day. So, if you think you're not good enough, you're probably not."

Her words cut through me. "I don't decide anything. I didn't choose this."

"So, you have no control over your life or how you live it?" Fire flashed in her eyes.

I gritted my teeth in frustration. "I'm doing the best I can."

That softened her expression a little. "Tell me something. If you could do anything . . . be anything, what would you be?"

"Free," I bit out the word.

Her eyes widened, then she nodded. "Then you need to find a way to be."

"It's not that easy."

She pursed her lips. "I know, but what's the alternative?"

I was living the alternative, and it wasn't something I was proud of. "You're really okay with painting?"

Chapter Twelve

Megan

A SHORT TIME later, dressed in sleep shorts and a T-shirt, I was standing on a stepladder painting the wooden trim around a sliding glass door. Although I had no prior experience in construction, Ollie's attention to detail was impressive. The walls were smooth and the lines where one color met another were straight and crisp. He was a perfectionist, and I hoped the amount the person who'd hired him was paying matched the level of quality he delivered. With that in mind, I painted slowly and meticulously, making sure I in no way detracted from his work. A thought occurred to me. "Did you say you built this with Levi?"

"He definitely helped."

I looked around in wonder. "It's flawless. You must work together well."

He kept painting the window trim. "We've been best friends for as long as I can remember. There's no one I trust more."

That's how I felt about Shelby. "There's nothing better than having someone who understands you even when you don't understand yourself."

He paused and turned to look at me. "Yeah."

"What's it like to live somewhere where everyone knows everyone else so well?"

With a grimace, he tipped his head to the side. "My answer would depend on the day you ask, I guess. I've never lived anywhere else, so I have nothing to compare it to, but there are times when I wish people knew a little less about me."

"Living in a city would give you that. Sometimes I wonder how long it would take someone to find my body if I woke up dead one day."

"Woke up dead?"

"You know what I mean."

"I'm sure one of your boyfriends would notice when you don't show up for dinner."

"Was that a dig?" I asked with a chuckle.

His smirk was telling. "Of course not."

Smiling, I resumed painting. "Well, you held up your side of the bargain, so ask me anything. My life is an open book."

"How many?"

"What?"

"Men are you dating?"

"What's your definition of dating?"

After a pause, he said, "Fucking."

"None." I thought about the last time I'd gotten lonely enough to say yes to a man. "At least, not for a few months."

"Okay." A glance in his direction confirmed he'd returned to painting as well. "How many of the men who feed you have you fucked?"

"That's a direct question."

"You did say I could ask anything."

I did. "Two?"

"You're not sure?"

"Two."

"Out of?"

"Five?"

"Are you asking me or telling me?"

I chewed my lip while pushing back any embarrassment. "I don't like to eat alone nor do these guys. Like I said, some I'm in a quasi-relationship with and some are just friends who like to feed me."

"No, all of them want to be in a relationship with you and be fucking you, but only two partially succeeded."

I frowned. "I am very clear with boundaries. They're friends."

He shook his head. "Who feed you."

My patience started to fade. "I don't ask them to."

"I'm sure you don't." After a pause, he asked, "How often do you see these men?"

I hesitated. "You're going to judge me."

"Maybe." His eyes darkened as he looked at me with an intensity that was unsettling. "But tell me anyway."

"I see Steve every Monday because he visits his mother on Sundays, and she has dementia. That makes him sad. So, we meet up on Mondays for Italian food and I cheer him up."

"By fucking him?"

I laughed at that. "No. By listening. He runs a small pharmaceutical company, and it kills him that nothing so far has been able to help his mother."

"Is he one of the ones you were with?"

I tipped my head to the side. "Yes. How did you know?"

"Tell me about the next guy."

"I see Joel on Tuesdays. He's been divorced for a few years and spends most of his free time with his kids, but never has them on Tuesdays. That makes him sad. He's a vegetarian so we try out different places that have food he can eat."

"And he always pays?"

"He won't even let me take out my wallet."

"Does he know about Steve?"

I shrugged. "I've been clear with him that we're only friends."

"I see." Ollie placed his paintbrush on the cover of the paint can. "Who do you see on Wednesday?"

The conversation didn't appear to be bothering him, so why not share? "Arnie is a professional bodybuilder." I smiled as I thought about how ridiculously huge he was. "He's enormous but surprisingly shy. We met once when I thought I might want to exercise on a regular basis, but turns out, I'm more of an eater than an athlete."

Ollie didn't laugh at my joke. "Who's Thursday?"

"Cole. He's brilliant but has a difficult time interacting with people. He loves Indian food and so do I. Whenever he has a big charity or social event, we meet up and I help him practice what he'll say. We met at a party. He looked so scared . . ."

"You fucked him."

I made a pained face. "Just once."

"I see." Ollie folded his arms across his chest. "And Friday?"

"Bryant. His wife died in a car accident several years ago. He hates to go places alone, but he doesn't want to be in a relationship because he thinks women just want to be with him for his money."

"But you just want the food."

"Do you want me to stop sharing?" I threw an empty paper towel roll at Ollie. He sidestepped it easily.

"No, I want to know. But which one of these men do you think is not in love with you?"

I got down from the stepladder and mirrored his pose. "All of them. I don't know what you're imagining I do with them, but we just meet up, have a meal, a few laughs, then each go home in our own cars. I like it because I like people and they're all absolute gentlemen. They like it because I don't ask them for anything and—"

"You're gorgeous."

I made a face and shook my head. "Sure. I'm short, fluffy, and if I'm not careful with the sun my face breaks out in freckles each summer. Cute, yes. Gorgeous?"

He lowered his arms and walked toward me with an expression that nearly had me retreating, but I held my ground. When he was directly in front of me, he tipped my chin upward and studied my face. "Who did you date before these guys?"

I swallowed hard and answered in a hoarse tone, "Someone who broke my heart."

He nodded. "I'm sorry."

I had never felt more seen and understood. "It's okay. It's been a while."

"What did he do?"

"Lied about everything, especially about being faithful. Then wasn't even there for me when I needed him."

"He hurt you badly, didn't he?"

"He did."

"These men you're seeing think they can access your heart, but you've got that tightly closed off, don't you?"

"I don't make them any promises."

"But do you tell them what you just told me?"

"They don't ask."

Time suspended. "If you were mine, I wouldn't share

you."

"I don't need a man's permission to do anything."

"You'd need mine," he growled and bent until his breath heated my lips. "Luckily I'm not looking for a relationship."

"Me neither," I said without much conviction.

He ran a hand through my hair. "I don't want to be your Saturday."

"Good," I said in a thick voice. "I don't need another part-time man."

The way he looked at me, like I was something he'd like to devour, sent fireworks exploding through me. When his hand burrowed into the hair on the nape of my neck, I shivered with anticipation.

"Cold?" he asked. His free hand ran up and down my bare arm.

I stood there, knowing this was a bad idea, but also drawn to him beyond what I could deny. "The exact opposite."

His eyes widened with pleasure, and I felt the heady rush of knowing he was as turned on as I was. I pressed a hand against the ladder behind me to steady myself, and he moved in closer. I met his mouth halfway, and our kiss was everything I'd imagined the right one would feel like.

This wasn't the brief caress of his lips over mine. No, this time, he was taking what I was offering and with a boldness that had me melting against him. I opened my mouth to his tongue, and he hauled me closer to him as he left me with no question of how he felt. His cock was bulging against the front of his jeans and as we kissed, I writhed against it, loving how he moaned when I did.

My hands took on a life of their own, exploring every inch of him they could reach and tugging at any clothing that stood between them and him. He kissed his way from my mouth to my neck and down the center of my chest. His breath warmed the material of my shirt in the most delicious way until I couldn't bear another moment of being clothed. When I reached for the edge of my shirt, preparing to haul it up and over my head, he took both of my wrists in his hands. "I like you, Megan."

I didn't understand the confusion in his eyes. "I like you too."

"You deserve better than this."

Lust and pride battled within me. "So, you're not a good fuck?" It wasn't a kind thing to say, but I wasn't feeling kind. I was teetering on a mistake I was eager to make, and he was forcing me to consider if it was a wise choice. I didn't want to think—I wanted to *feel*.

"That's all it would be."

Angry with him for stealing the beauty of the experience from me, I said, "If you don't shut up, I'll go find someone who can do this without making me feel bad about myself."

His face tightened. "I never want you to feel bad about anything you do with me."

I was starting to, and I hated that the best thing I'd felt

with a man was beginning to feel like the worst. I shook my head and began to pull away.

It was the wrong thing to say if my goal had been to build something meaningful with him. But it was the right thing to say if I wanted him to put aside whatever his reservations were and give himself over totally to the passion rocking through both of us.

He whipped my shirt up and over my head with a force that would have scared me had I not already been so turned on. With fire burning in his eyes, he stripped me bare, then made short work of removing his own clothing. I could barely breathe by the time he stepped out of his jeans and tossed them aside. His cock waved in the air, large and confident.

My sex clenched in anticipation.

"Do you know what ladder sex is?" he asked.

"Sex on a ladder?" There was one behind me. It made sense.

His grin was a pure carnal promise. "No, it's when you do as much to each other as you can before either of you come. How long do you think you could last?"

"I have no idea." God, usually I was glad if I came at all. Nothing like this had ever been offered to me before. My voice came out in a whisper. "But I wouldn't mind finding out."

He ran the back of his fingers across the side of one of my breasts. "There are four steps. If you come before the last one, the winner gets to decide how they'd like to come, and you have to agree."

"Have to?"

His roaming hand spread across my stomach then dipped lower to cup my sex. "Within reason. I'd never play a game where the word no wasn't an option."

Thank God. "Okay."

He dipped his middle finger between my folds and began to move it back and forth over my clit. "Step one: one of us goes down on the other until told to stop."

"Stop?" I was having difficulty focusing, but that was probably his goal. He bent and nipped at one of my rock-hard nipples.

"If you don't stop before you come, you lose."

I writhed against his hand. "And that's bad."

"Oh, yes." His finger moved to my opening and thrust deeply within. "It ends the game. And the longer you wait the better the orgasm is."

"Right." So, there was something better than closing my eyes and praying my partner didn't finish before I did? "That makes sense."

"Step two: we change places. If you were going down on me, it's my turn to go down on you."

Normal breathing was no longer possible. "Sounds fair."

"The steps continue until asked to stop."

"Okay."

"We take turns saying what we want, but we stop before

the release, and we see who gets the highest up the ladder."

His finger pumped in and out of my sex with an expertise that already had me wondering if I wasn't going to lose before we even started the game. "Who goes first?" I asked thickly.

He brushed his lips over mine and murmured. "You choose."

Only the fear that his tongue was as talented as his fingers held me back from spreading my legs for him. I wanted to experience something better than I had. "I'll go down on you."

He smiled and put a hand on my shoulder. "Then get on your knees."

I lowered myself before him and loved how he took command of my head. Hands deep in my hair, he plunged his cock into my mouth. I had to stretch to accommodate both the length and girth of him.

As I tried to remember the best techniques I'd tried out over the years, he made most of my moves impossible as he fucked my mouth so deeply, I would have gagged had he not stopped just short of that depth. Still, there was no tenderness, and I didn't want any. I dug my hands into his bare ass and opened my mouth wider, swirled my tongue around him more forcefully. His breathing became ragged, and I tasted his precum just before he said, "Stop," and pulled out.

Without giving me time to decide if it was a good idea or not, he lifted me off the ground and sat me on the top of the ladder. When it wobbled beneath me, I squeaked, but in an instant, he whipped my legs over his shoulders and I clung to the sides of the ladder as he plundered my sex with his tongue.

He teased me by flicking back and forth over my clit. He thrust inside me with his impossibly long tongue. When he brought a hand up to work in tandem with his mouth, I shuddered, it was so damn good. Were we in a bed? On a cloud? I couldn't have told you because I'd stepped outside my body to a place where everything felt so good I didn't want to ever go back.

His mouth and fingers found a rhythm that sent a wave of warmth through me. I tried to stop it. I bit my lip and told myself to hold off, but it was too powerful. I should have told him to stop, but I needed this release more than I needed air. I gave myself over to it and let out a sob that I quickly tried to disguise as a cough.

He didn't ask me if I came.

Was it so wrong if I didn't tell him? I mean, it's not like there were referees in this game that could call foul. "Stop," I said, huskily. Not feeling bad at all that he didn't appear to notice I'd already lost.

He wiped his mouth on the back of his hand, then lowered me back to my feet. "Turn around," he ordered. "And hold onto the ladder." As I turned, he dug into the pocket of his jeans, pulled out a condom, and rolled it on.

HE THRUST INSIDE me so hard and so deep I gasped and braced myself. Lord, he was huge. It was too much, but then it was fucking perfect. I was wet and he was unrestrained. The sex I'd had with others hadn't prepared me for this . . . claiming. Everyone had felt like practice for the real thing and in no way in the same league.

He drove harder, faster, deeper.

It was glorious.

He paused. "You have to be close," he growled.

Oh, I was, but I had a theory to test. "Don't stop."

He kept going, gloriously powerful. Another orgasm rose within me, and I told myself I should announce it or tell him to stop, but I couldn't. Surely, I'd die if I didn't let myself have this. Hands gripping the sides of the ladder, I held in all sounds that would have revealed when I gave myself over to a second, even more powerful wave of pleasure. When I finally had some semblance of sanity back, I tried to sound near out of control and said, "Stop."

He withdrew with a swear. Gasping for air, he said, "I was so close."

"Me too," I lied, trying not to smile. "So now I get to choose?"

"Yes."

I looked around the room. There wasn't much beyond construction supplies. "You think you could hold me?"

"I'm sure I could."

I stepped backward and up a few steps of the ladder. His

hands came to my waist to lift me toward him. I wrapped my legs around him and felt the first nudge of his cock against my sex. Already partially sated, I wasn't in a rush. I pulled his head back down to mine and kissed him deeply. Everything about him felt good, tasted good. Bare chest to bare chest, I could have lived there forever.

He walked with me a few steps, until my back rested against one of the walls. Only then he thrust upward and into me. It was—mind scrambling. I moved with him, welcoming each thrust, and meeting it with as much enthusiasm. Our hands weren't gentle. Our kisses turned to nips. His mouth savored every curve and tip he could reach as he drove up into me.

"I'm going to come," he growled into my ear.

The last thing I thought before I let myself join him was that he might be wrong about how holding off made an orgasm better. I hadn't and my third was by far my best, not just of the day, but of my life. It rocked me to my very soul and left me shattered and clinging to him.

Chapter Thirteen

Ollie

STILL BREATHING RAGGEDLY, I lowered Megan to the floor. Sex with someone I hardly knew wasn't a new experience for me. Long winters in Maine made partnering up nearly as recreational as skiing. We were smart enough to choose people from out of town, but Megan's concern that I would judge her was unfounded.

The person I was judging was myself. I didn't like that she had other men in her life. I didn't like how much I wanted what had just happened between us to mean something. Confused, I kissed her on the forehead and turned away to clean off.

The reality of where we were didn't match the way I felt about her. Our first time should have been somewhere special, something we could look back on . . . My hands fisted. I was being stupid. She wasn't in Driverton to stay, and I was not in a good place in my life. I picked up her clothing and handed it to her before gathering up my own.

We carefully kept from looking each other in the eye as we dressed. Normally, this was when I'd promise to call and, if the sex was good enough, I would. But this sex had been phenomenal. The kind of sex that makes a man wonder if he'll ever find another woman attractive again. Nothing I'd normally say felt right.

Fully dressed again, I could no longer bear the silence. "I'm not sorry that happened."

"I'm not either," she said quietly.

I turned and raised my eyes to hers. Hair tousled, cheeks glowing, she was so beautiful I forgot what I intended to say and raised a hand to cup her cheek. "I wish—"

She laid her hand over mine. "Don't. I have a theory that nothing anyone says after those two words should ever be voiced. In life you either do something or you don't. Wishing things were different doesn't change anything and only makes people sad."

Her words hit so true they hurt. "I'm not in a good place right now. I don't like my life. I don't like myself. I like you, but you wouldn't like me for long if you chose to be with me right now." God, that sounded lame.

I expected her to ask me what the hell I was trying to say, but she gave my hand a squeeze and removed it from her face, releasing it to drop at my side. "Then don't wish—do, and maybe you'll become someone we can both imagine me being with."

"I wish—" I stopped there. "Okay." Remembering how

much working with Bradford had helped Everette, I vowed to give that path a second chance.

Neither of us spoke for several awkward moments.

She gave my shoulder a shove. "Don't look so glum, the sex was so good I cheated."

A smile pulled at my lips. "You came and didn't tell me?"

She shrugged and batted her eyelashes at me. "I figured if you couldn't tell, why should I?"

Looking back, there'd definitely been signs, but I'd been too out of my mind to put much thought into anything beyond not exploding and losing. "We will definitely need a rematch."

"Someday." She winked and my gut clenched. I wanted to haul her to me and announce all kinds of insane things to her: she could no longer see other men, I would change for her, and she was mine.

But I didn't.

I tapped her nose with a finger instead. "Are you hungry?"

"Always."

"Want to go to Little Willie's and grab lunch?"

Her smile was genuine. "I'd love that."

We quickly closed the paint and washed the brushes. The drive to Little Willie's was surprisingly comfortable. I asked her how she'd spent the day before and she told me all about it. The sound of her voice brought a feeling of peace that I'd yearned for.

I wasn't ready for her—nor did I want to lose her. "I'd like to stay in touch."

She shot me a side glance. "That would be nice."

Nice wasn't how I imagined it would go. Detrimental to my ability to date other women? Yes. Frustrating? Absolutely. Nice? No. More like a torture I was choosing to inflict upon myself.

Chapter Fourteen

Megan

SEATED ACROSS FROM my Thursday dinner date, Cole, at our favorite Indian restaurant, I took a sip of mango lassi and smiled. It had taken me a few weeks to not get emotional every time I thought about Ollie, but time and distance had helped.

My life was back on track and there was a comfort in that. Cole was telling me about a small business he had just acquired, and I felt bad that my thoughts kept wandering.

"You're thinking about him again," Cole said without looking upset about it.

He and I were friends so there was no need to lie. "Yes."

"Did he text you?"

I shook my head. "Not for weeks."

There was only compassion in Cole's eyes as he took a bite of his butter chicken. After a moment, he said, "Have you considered contacting him? If you're still thinking about him, you're obviously interested."

I let out a sigh. "I am and I'm not. In person, we had a strong connection, and the chemistry was off the charts, but when we tried to stay in touch . . ."

"Is he crude?"

"No. Not at all. We spoke on the phone a few times. He asked me all about my life here and told me about his. There's so much I like about him."

"For instance?"

"He's a humble caretaker of people. Everyone I've spoken to in Driverton says he takes after his father in that respect. He's a hard worker and often the first person to step up and help when anyone needs something."

"Those are rare characteristics."

"He does so much for so many people—without expecting anything in return. I've told you about Little Willie's."

"You have."

"It devours all the money he makes, but he doesn't ask anyone to help him fund it. And he could. There are several people in that town now who are wealthy. If he told them about his situation, I bet they'd contribute."

"He sounds too proud for that."

"He is."

"And you admire that about him."

"I do. He's strong in a way that isn't flashy. And he has integrity. If you talk to anyone in Driverton, they'll tell you a story about something he's done for them. He won't tell you himself."

"And yet you don't sound happy when you talk about him or interested in reaching out to him."

"He drinks." I wrinkled my nose. "A lot."

Cole finished another bite of his chicken. "That's a red flag."

"I know." Remembering what Ollie had said about all my male friends secretly being in love with me, I tipped my head to the side. "Could I ask you something?"

"Anything."

"Are you and I friends?"

He smiled. "That's a funny question to ask someone you see every week."

"Does it bother you that I'm talking about another man?"

"Do I look bothered?"

He didn't. "I don't consider what we're doing dating."

"I have no issue with that."

"You and I had sex."

There was a twinkle in his eyes as he nodded. "I remember."

"I wish I believed I could help him quit drinking."

"I wouldn't sign up for such a job."

"You and I moved past sex to friendship. If I could do that with him, his drinking wouldn't be an issue."

"But?"

"I don't know why, but every time I think about being his friend it makes me sad."

Cole's eyes darkened. "Not every relationship is meant to be."

I laid a hand over his. "Do I make you sad?"

This time his smile didn't reach his eyes. "Not until recently. Thursdays with you have consistently brought me joy. You've been a beacon of kindness and positivity in my otherwise stress-filled and cutthroat life."

I made a pained face. "Until I started talking about Ollie."

His hand turned beneath mine. "I hoped you and I would one day be more than we are, but you've been so good to me for so long that all I want is to see you happy."

It felt like a breakup even though we'd never said we were dating. "I'm sorry."

"Don't be." His smile returned even as he let my hand go. "I didn't see any harm in taking you out each week, but I think it kept both of us in limbo. The possibility of you was enough to keep me from looking for anything more. And you may not want to see it but having dinner with me each week is holding you back as well. It might be time for us to let each other go."

"Why does that scare me?" I asked myself but voiced it aloud.

"I don't have the answer to that question, but maybe the men you see the rest of the week will."

My mouth rounded at his snark as well as the surprise that he knew about the others. "Wait, how do you know what I do when I'm not with you?"

"I've made it my business to."

"How long have you known?"

"Since the first time I asked you if you were busy on a Monday and you said you were busy for all of them."

I mulled that. "So you always knew?"

He nodded.

"If it didn't bother you, why is talking about a man I'm not seeing an issue?"

"Because this one touched your heart. I see it in your eyes whenever you talk about him."

Is that what Ollie had done? Touched my heart? If so, why didn't that feel good? "So, no more Thursdays?"

He took my hand in his, brought it to his mouth, and kissed my knuckles. "If you ever need me, I'm only a phone call away. If, while we are apart, you miss me, you know where I am. But don't come to me just because you don't want to be alone. We both deserve better."

I almost said, "I wish things could be different," but I really did believe that not much good came after the words *I wish*. In an attempt to lighten the mood, I said, "Does this mean you'll finally allow me to pay for a meal?"

"Never." He released my hand. "Eat your damn samosa chaat before I do. I'm going to miss it almost as much as I'll miss you." He winked to soften his words, making me sad that I didn't feel more than friendship for him.

We ended the night just outside the restaurant with a

hug that lasted longer than usual. He murmured, "If he's not good to you, don't give him your heart."

"I won't." It was an easy promise to make. I'd only opened my heart once and the pain of realizing I'd meant nothing to that man was something I wasn't ready to open myself to anytime soon. "I'm not even sure I can."

When he stepped back, there was goodbye in his eyes. "Take care of yourself."

"You too."

And just like that I had Thursdays to myself again.

Chapter Fifteen

Megan

BACK IN MY apartment, I kicked off my shoes near the door and headed to my bedroom to change. On my way, I stopped and bent to say hello to Myrtle who was basking in the warmth of her sunlamp. She was a Reeves turtle and my first pet.

My phone buzzed with an incoming call. *Shelby.* I answered while continuing to my bedroom. "Hey, you."

"Everyone is fine, but you won't believe what happened today." Shelby had had an emotional year, so the higher-than-normal pitch to her voice was . . . well, now normal.

I stripped down and sighed at the comfort of my favorite knee-length flannel sleepshirt. "I'm ready—spill."

"First, I'm calling you from urgent care. Everette is getting stitches on his head."

"I thought you said everyone is fine. That doesn't sound fine."

"Alive, we're all alive. That's what I meant."

"Wait, what did I miss? Were you in an accident?"

"No, nothing so tame."

As I padded back to my living room, my patience began to thin. "I've had a long day, could you just tell me please?" Grabbing a thick blanket, I curled up on my couch and covered myself with it.

"Are you okay?"

"I'm fine. Nothing worth mentioning, I'm just tired. Go on."

"Okay, well it started earlier today when Cooper and Tom came into Little Willie's and told Everette they had a job for him. There's a town south of Driverton where people have been going missing, and Bradford was hired to locate a woman whose last known location was that area."

"Holy shit." I hugged the blanket to myself.

"I thought it was too dangerous. I begged Everette not to go, but he said he had to, although he promised to call me every hour on the hour, and he never breaks a promise. So when he missed a call, I knew something had happened to him."

"Oh, my God."

"Katie, Levi, and Ollie were at Little Willie's. I told them I knew Everette was in real danger. I don't know how I knew, but I did. And they believed me. We headed out together to find him."

"You should have called me."

"There was no time. We came across a little restaurant

and guessed he would have stopped there. Ollie and Levi had their shotguns with them, so we decided to find out for ourselves."

"Hold on, Ollie and Levi have shotguns?"

"I'm pretty sure everyone in Driverton does. Anyway, there was blood outside the restaurant, and it looked like someone was dragged inside. I was freaking out."

"Of course, you were."

"Katie picked the lock. Levi and Ollie went inside. Tyr went to the cooler door, where we found Everette. He and the woman he was sent to find were tied up in there. Tied up. And he was all bloody. I'm never going to be able to get the image of that out of my head."

"And then what happened?"

"Everette told us the restaurant was run by serial killers and told us to leave him, but that would never happen. You should have seen how brave Ollie and Levi were. When Ollie said those people fucked up when they took someone from Driverton . . . I know this sounds insane because we were all very much still in danger . . . but that was one of the first times I've felt *safe* since losing my parents. Levi, Ollie, and Everette—they're family, you know? Not blood, but by something deeper. I knew they wouldn't let anything happen to me."

I shivered as I realized how differently this conversation might have gone. "Did they catch the killers? Is the woman okay?"

"They sure did catch them. If I could have taken a photo of the condition we left them in, I would have, but none of us can speak of that outside our circle."

"Why?"

"We didn't call the police."

"Hold on, all this happened, and no one notified the police?"

"Bradford showed up and handled everything."

"Oh, okay. So they're in government custody."

"Something like that."

I'd met Bradford in person, and although he seemed nice enough, he definitely wasn't someone I'd want to cross. "So, Everette is getting stitches . . . was anyone else hurt?" I didn't want to ask about Ollie specifically. Shelby and I usually told each other everything, but although I'd told her I'd enjoyed my day out with him, I'd left out one important aspect of that day. Why? I couldn't say. When it came to Ollie I was all kinds of confused.

"Thankfully it was only Everette and his injuries are minor. He has a concussion, and he lost a good amount of blood, but he'll be fine. They're not keeping him overnight. I'm not sure, though, if it's because he's okay to go home or if he's too stubborn to stay. Either way, I'm so grateful we found him in time."

"Yeah." My thoughts were a jumble of fear and relief. The last time she'd called me about a criminal with bad intentions there'd been no good news. The man who'd broken into her parents' home had not only tried to rob them, but had died in a fire along with them.

I tortured myself by imagining how I would have felt had this call included news that Ollie was gone. Dead. Senselessly, the same way Shelby had lost her parents.

If I didn't want to be with him, why did the idea of never seeing him again gut me?

"Are you okay, Megan?" Shelby asked.

It was only then I realized my breathing had turned ragged. I took a deep, calming breath. "Sorry, I'm so glad everyone's okay."

"We're gathering tonight at Everette's house to celebrate surviving today. I wish you lived closer."

"Me too."

"Megan, Levi just came to get me. We can see Everette now, so I have to go. I'll call you tomorrow."

"Tell him I'm glad he's okay."

"I will."

"And I'll come see you soon to celebrate you surviving too."

She laughed. "I'd love that. Bye."

She hung up.

"Bye."

I grabbed the pillow I kept on my couch, lay back, and tucked it beneath my head. I wanted to text Ollie so bad I kept picking up my phone. If we were still messaging back and forth, I would have, but it had been weeks since I'd heard from him. *Weeks.*

It wasn't like I'd never see him again. The next time I visited Shelby, even if I stayed at a hotel far outside of town, we'd still run into each other at Little Willie's.

If he were anyone else, I wouldn't wait—I'd just reach out.

I don't get awkward around men, not even the few I've had sex with. My parents were so judgmental that I try to look at myself with kinder eyes. *I don't regret anything I did with Ollie.*

Not even if that's all we ever have.

If I kept telling myself that, the ache I felt whenever I thought about him would eventually fade.

I must have dozed because the buzz of my phone woke me. I fumbled for it and answered without checking the caller ID. "Yes?"

"It's me, Ollie."

I sat up so fast the blanket hit the floor. I hurriedly recovered it. "Ollie."

He cleared his throat. "I know we haven't spoken in a while, but I wanted to hear your voice."

My throat thickened with emotion. "Did something happen?" Should I admit to knowing? Shelby had said it shouldn't be talked about outside their circle. Was I considered in that circle?

"Yeah, something happened. I'm sure Shelby will tell you all about it."

"Shelby? Not you?"

Rather than answering that question, he said, "I think about you all the time."

"I think about you too."

"I did something today that made me feel good about myself. It wasn't all me and I didn't do all that much, but I felt proud in a way I haven't in a long time."

"And?"

"And you're the one I wanted to share that with."

My heart beat wildly in my chest and tears filled my eyes. "I'm glad you did."

"How've you been?"

"Good."

Neither of us spoke for a few long moments.

He broke the silence first. "Today made me rethink a lot of things. I'm going to give working with Bradford a second chance."

Was that a good thing? Before today I might have thought so, but Everette had almost been killed because of his association with him. "Shelby already told me about today. Are you sure that's what you want to do?"

"If I ever want to get ahead, I need more than side jobs. He's the only opportunity in town."

"There are other towns."

"I love Driverton, and I have responsibilities here."

"Little Willie's."

"And my mother."

"Driverton *is* a pretty amazing place." In my head a

quick fantasy sprouted in which he agreed and asked me if I'd ever consider relocating there.

But he didn't agree or ask me anything. Levi called to him, and he said, "I have to go, but it was really good talking to you."

"You too."

"I'll call you when things settle down."

I almost told him not to bother. The only thing keeping us in each other's lives was the fact that my best friend was in love with a good friend of his. I shouldn't have had sex with him. This would have been a lighthearted check-in had we not visited heaven together.

Instead, it was a sad shadow of what might have been.

And this is why I let no one near my heart.

This sucks.

"Sounds good. Night, Ollie."

I hung up first.

Chapter Sixteen

Ollie

MY THOUGHTS WERE all over the place after hanging up with Megan. I hadn't meant to call her. Levi, Katie, Shelby, and I were all at the hospital, waiting while Everette got stitches in his scalp. We were partially riding high on the win of bringing Everette home while simultaneously dealing with the reality of how close we'd come to losing him.

Violence didn't touch Driverton often. Sure we had occasional brawls with outsiders or loud disputes between neighbors, but serial killers? Not in my lifetime and, as far as I knew, not in the history of the town.

My stomach churned as I thought about how many people those two had killed. We'd put an end to that. Well, we'd played a part in stopping them. Bradford would carry the weight of whatever came next.

Everette credited working with Bradford for not only sobering him up but also putting him on a successful path. He certainly seemed to have his shit together.

And I needed to do something.

Still, when it came to working with Bradford, I had my reservations. There was so much we didn't know about him. Even Simon, Everette's cousin who was in the FBI, was closed-mouthed when it came to anything about Bradford.

I didn't doubt that the world needed someone like Bradford, but did Driverton? I wasn't as sold on him as my friends were. Yes, he rescued people, but there was a dark side to him that collectively we were choosing to overlook.

Never had any of us dealt with someone with so much blood on their hands. He was not only wealthy, but also deadly. What would someone like that do if any of us ever crossed him?

Levi and I discussed that while we drove my truck behind the others. He drummed his fingers on his knees. "After today, there's no way Katie won't want to train with Bradford."

"I agree. I don't trust him, but I'm willing to give him a second chance."

"Then I will as well."

My thoughts were chaotic, possibly because I'd stared serial killers in the face that day and won. "Levi, do you think you're not who you're meant to be?"

"I think about as little as possible as often as possible."

He wasn't entirely joking, and I didn't laugh. "Today, when we saved not only Everette but that woman they would have killed as well—I glimpsed a different version of myself."

"It is nice to know we made a difference."

"Then why do I feel like shit?" I didn't tell him I'd called Megan. He didn't know I'd been with her. Levi and I didn't keep much from each other, but Megan wasn't a conquest or a distraction. She wasn't a drunken mistake. I didn't know what she was, but I'd felt unsettled ever since I'd met her. "I'm not happy, Levi. Not with who I am. Not with what I'm doing with my life."

"Who the fuck is?" He grunted. "Besides Everette."

I did laugh at that one. "Good question."

We drove along without saying more and Megan once again filled my thoughts. It had felt so damn good to hear her voice. Too good.

Instead of going to Everette's, I wanted to drive to her. I wanted to ask her if she was still seeing anyone else, and if she was, I wanted to spend the whole night showing her why I was all she'd ever need.

Except I probably can't afford the amount of gas it would take to get to her.

I laughed without humor.

"You okay?" Levi asked. "Do you want me to drive?"

"I'm fine." Or I will be. A few drinks would take the edge off.

The next few hours went by in a pleasant enough blur. We all gathered at Everette's house and had a few beers. I may have had too many to remember exactly what we talked about, but two things stuck with me.

One: Clay Landon, Cooper's rich brother, wanted to

build some kind of Batman-style lair under Driverton. The details were a little fuzzy, but he tended to be more than a little over the top so I wouldn't put it past him.

Two: Much to my irritation, Shelby asked Clay if he had any single friends for Megan. Great, nothing would bring me more joy than to watch some rich jackass make a play for my—

My what? What was Megan to me? What did I want her to be?

Before I could give those questions serious consideration, I needed to make some real changes in my life. Stop drinking. Train with Bradford. Make enough money to put some aside for something crazy like flying out to see Megan and taking her out to dinner.

Chapter Seventeen

>>>><<<<

Megan

Two weeks later

"MY FULL NAME is Edward Alexander Charles Demande, Crown Prince of Rubare Collina." The tall man with dark hair and darker eyes bent until his face was mere inches from mine.

Had I known I'd be meeting royalty, I might have worn something better than a cotton, sleeveless summer dress. Of all the people gathered on Mrs. Williams's lawn to witness Everette proposing to Shelby, why had the best-dressed man there sought me out? "Megan."

His smile started in his eyes. "I'm well aware of who you are, Miss Gassett."

"You are?"

He dipped his head just a fraction closer. "Oh, yes. I don't make a habit of flying across the ocean to meet someone, but Clay Landon has known my father for a long time. How could my interest not be piqued by the first woman he's ever suggested worthy of marrying into our family?"

"Marrying?" I forced a bright smile. "Wow. That's a lot . . . and a huge honor?" I looked around quickly, spotting Clay in the crowd. Was this his idea of a practical joke? If so . . . ha ha? When I caught Clay's attention, his eyebrows rose and he nodded toward the prince as if saying, "He's great, isn't he?"

I let out a nervous laugh and gave the prince another once-over. Dressed in a dark blue suit with a green and gold sash beneath his jacket, he looked like he'd stepped out of a holiday romance where some quirky woman falls for a hot prince. If I had to guess, he was a few years younger than I was. Shouldn't my heart be racing? My face warming? By anyone's standards, he was above-average attractive. And rich.

Nothing.

I haven't felt a single flutter for anyone since meeting Ollie, and I was beginning to think that was a problem. Ollie wasn't interested in me, and nothing about us getting together made sense. I needed to get him out of my head.

Across a lawn where nearly everyone in Driverton was either on lawn chairs or seated at fancy tables Clay had brought in, I spotted Ollie. He was standing with Bradford, his wife, Levi and Katie. When our eyes met, he didn't look away.

Regardless of the physical distance between us, the air sizzled and my breath caught in my throat. In jeans and a plaid shirt, he was a thousand times more attractive than the man beside me.

I'm not the type who likes bad boys.

Ollie has issues and not a single one of them is my problem.

The prince's voice tore my attention from Ollie. "My country is an island kingdom. It has long been our custom to choose women from outside our borders."

"Choose." I swallowed hard. "Aren't you a little young to be thinking about marriage?"

"I am twenty and three." He placed a hand on my lower back, and I wasn't sure how I felt about his touch. "A man is never too young to lay claim to a good woman."

"Lay claim?" I laughed, but stopped abruptly when he didn't join in. After clearing my throat, I said, "I'm a couple years older than you are. Sadly, probably too old."

"Do not worry, purity is no longer a requirement in choosing a royal bride in Rubare Collina."

I coughed. "Thank goodness for that." With a shift of my body, I moved away from his touch. The act seemed to increase his interest in me. "It has been such an . . . honor to meet you. I should probably—"

"Are you intimidated by me, little American?"

I raised a finger in request for him to stop. "First, okay, I am short, but you don't need to call my attention to that. I'm well aware of it every time I go shopping and need to ask for assistance to get anything above the third shelf. Second, I'm not princess material. This is as fancy as I get, and I didn't even paint my toenails. I meant to, but I forgot."

His laugh was a little patronizing. "You are a delight."

I shook my head. "Thank you. That's kind of you to say."

"Clay mentioned you enjoyed your rides in his helicopter."

"I did," I said with a smile as memories from those two rides returned. "I mean, who doesn't love a luxury helicopter, am I right?"

"I agree. It would be my pleasure to take you out tomorrow in one of my own. Name the place and I'll make the arrangements for it to happen."

I don't know what came over me. I spontaneously said, "The Egyptian pyramids."

"Done, although that would require a flight in a jet first, but I always keep one fueled up and nearby."

"I was joking," I said weakly and glanced around for help. "Oh, look, Everette and Shelby are kissing. He must have just proposed. And I missed it. Darn it. I should head over there and congratulate them."

"What time should I pick you up for our trip tomorrow?" There was a look in his eyes that had me laughing nervously.

"I'm sorry. I need to take a rain check on that. My best friend just got engaged, and that means I'll be busy. So busy. Crazy busy. For a while. But thank you. This was . . . great. And I hope you and Clay have a wonderful time catching up."

"Run if you must, little American, but you'll hear from

me again."

I waved to him over my shoulder as I hastily strode away. Reana joined me and fell into step beside me. "Clay must like you if he flew in a royal for you."

My pace slowed and I wrinkled my nose. "I didn't ask him to."

"I didn't think you did."

I glanced back at the prince who winked at me when he caught me looking. "I'm sure he's someone's type, just not mine."

"Would you like me to keep him away from you?"

I stopped and met her gaze. "What would you do?"

"There are a few older widows in this town who'd love the chance to talk to any single man, even if he is half their age. I'll call in a favor and they won't leave his side unless his security team hauls them away. Mrs. Green has a walker. They wouldn't dare touch her. And Mrs. Cashel has an electric scooter. He can't outrun her."

"I couldn't ask them to do that." I laughed into my hand. "That's so awful."

"They'd love every moment of it."

I really didn't want to be cornered by the prince again. "Okay. Tell the ladies thank you and I'll owe them a big favor for this."

Reana smiled. "I will."

I hugged her. "I'm going to congratulate Shelby and Everette then find somewhere to sit. At least now I won't have to hide."

When Reana stepped back from my embrace, she said, "In Driverton, we take care of our own."

My eyes blurred with tears. Sure, I was staying in the same house as a man who was making himself scarce just because we'd accidentally fucked, but maybe that didn't mean I couldn't make this town my home away from home. I was already getting attached to people there. When I'd arrived late the night before, Reana had greeted me like visiting family. She and Shelby had stayed up with me, talking through most of the night. It was the uncomplicated, warm welcome I'd often wished for from my parents. "Thank you."

She waved my gratitude off but was smiling as she headed toward a table of white-haired ladies. I delivered a long hug to Shelby and her giant fiancé, then sought out a seat at a small table partially hidden by a hedge.

Alone with my thoughts, I gave myself a firm mental shake. Not only had Ollie robbed me of a chance to wear a crown, but he was single-handedly ruining my social life. The only reason he had the power to? Because I couldn't stop comparing how I felt with anyone else to how I felt with him.

Work boots entered my vision. My eyes flew upward to meet Ollie's.

"Mind if I sit down?"

I should say no. I should tell him I'm busy planning my trip to Egypt. "Sure."

He sat in the chair next to me, so close I had to fight not to lean closer and see if he smelled as good as I remembered. After drumming his fingers on his knee, he said, "Won't your date miss you if you're hiding back here?"

"I don't have a date." My chin rose and I looked away.

"Not even the prince Clay flew in for you?"

The humor in his voice was grating. "No comment."

He smirked. "No need. If you liked him, you wouldn't be back here hiding."

"Unless I'm playing hard to get."

That wiped the smile from his face. "Are you?"

I took a deep breath. "It's none of your business, is it?"

He made a sound deep in his throat. "I've missed you."

Nope. I wasn't letting him in. "Really, that must be why you called me so often. Oh, wait, you didn't . . ."

"I wanted to."

"If you wanted to, you would have."

"Neither of us is ready for more."

I searched his face and hated how strong our connection still was. I felt his pain and confusion so acutely it might have been my own. I didn't need to ask him what he meant. I knew. "Speak for yourself."

"You still letting men you're not interested in feed you?"

"You still getting drunk all the time?"

He laughed without humor. "We're quite the pair, aren't we?"

Remorse for what I'd said came quick. "I shouldn't have

said what I did about you drinking."

"I'm not offended. I drink—more than I should. It gets me through the day. I intend to quit, though. What about you?"

"I already don't drink . . . not much anyway."

"I wasn't referring to alcohol."

"Then I have no idea what you're talking about."

"I've been thinking about these men you see once a week."

"Please don't feel you need to share those thoughts with me."

"You don't come across as someone who likes to be the center of attention."

He was right about that, but I wasn't going to admit anything and encourage him.

He continued, "You've slotted them all neatly into the category of friends."

I folded my arms across my chest. "Because they are my friends."

"Are they, though? Or are you only using them to fill space in your life?"

My lips pressed together in anger before I said, "I'm so glad we met. Before you I didn't have anyone who could make me feel bad about myself in so few words."

He sighed. "Is that what I'm doing? I'm sorry." He moved to stand.

I should have let him go. "Ollie."

"Yes?"

"I'm not using them, but they do fill a space in my life."

He sat back down. "I know."

"I don't like to be alone." God, why did I admit that aloud? It sounded pathetic.

"We all do what we have to do to survive." He ran a hand through my hair. "I know what my demons are. What are yours?"

"I don't ask myself questions I know I won't like the answer to. I'd rather focus on happy things."

"I understand that feeling well." He reached out and laced his fingers with mine. My heart thudded and my breathing shallowed. "If I had my own shit together I'd probably know how to help you with yours."

We exchanged a smile that warmed me to my soul. "Ditto."

"I'm determined to make real improvements in my life."

My mouth twisted in a half smile. "I've already broken up with three of the five guys I wasn't dating."

He whistled. "Three. You're already making better progress than I am. Which ones got the boot?"

"It wasn't solely my decision, but Steve, Joel, and Cole."

"Monday, Tuesday and Thursday."

My eyes widened. "You've got a good memory."

His smile was a little sad. "When it's something I care about. What happened?"

I looked away. "You don't want to hear this."

He gave my hand a squeeze. "I do, actually."

"Cole didn't like hearing so much about you." I wagged a finger at Ollie. "Don't read into that."

The corners of his eyes crinkled. "Never."

"You were right about them. They were hoping for more. Cole was upfront about that. When I told Steve and Joel about Cole's decision they decided dinners with me were no longer a good idea."

"And the other two?"

"Arnie doesn't care. He said I'm his arm candy chicklet. Not sure how I feel about that."

"That's a lie. You do know."

I did. I didn't like it, but it wasn't easy to sweep my social calendar clean. "I do. I've already decided to tell him it's over." Not because of Ollie, but also not *not* because of Ollie.

"What about Bryant?"

Ollie really did have a good memory. "I don't know what to say to him. He already lost his wife."

"It's kinder than leading him on."

"That's not what I'm doing. We laugh together. I do care about him." I looked down at my fingers laced with Ollie's. "You're changing the way I see things and I'm not sure I like it."

"I know exactly what you mean. I tell myself we don't make sense and you're better off without me." He ran his free hand through my hair again. "Then I see you . . ."

The brush of his lips over mine was enough to empty all rational thoughts from my head. Nothing mattered beyond the need filling me. I didn't want it. I couldn't have explained it. But it was there—a pulsing ache for him that couldn't be denied.

It wasn't a long kiss, but it left us both breathing raggedly. I told myself not to do it. I told myself once was enough. "Want to get out of here?" I asked breathlessly.

Hand in hand, like children released from class to recess, we sprinted away from the party and down a path that led into a wooded area. When I stumbled, Ollie stopped, bent over and motioned for me to hop onto his back. Without hesitation, I hiked up my skirt and climbed onto him. When he straightened, I tightened my legs around his waist and my arms around his neck.

His stride was powerful and sure, down winding dirt paths and up the side of a steep hill. He stepped out of the wooded area into a clearing that opened to the edge of a river at the base of a twenty-or-so-foot thin waterfall cascading down between two steep rock walls. I gasped at the beauty of it.

"Of course Driverton has a waterfall," I joked.

"A small one. We named it Dead Man's Chasm to keep the interest in it low. It's fed by mountain water and is a tributary to Dead River where the river expands and whitewater rafting becomes possible. In the spring, this area can be dangerous as the mountain caps melt, but this time of year you never see more than a light flow."

As he lowered me to my feet, I asked, "So no one actually died here?"

"Depends on who you ask. We'll tell outsiders whatever horror stories are necessary to limit interest in the area. If you ask those in neighboring towns, it's been everything from a murder site to contaminated with chemicals from the old mill. My personal favorite was the rumor my mother spread when some young people stumbled upon the site. They wanted to camp here and share the spot on their social media. My mother told them it was infested with mosquitos carrying the Chikungunya virus. None of us knew what that was, but she had us taking turns walking around, stooping over, and complaining that our joints hurt. I guess there's no cure for it, you just have to ride it out. Everette pretended to foam at the mouth at one point. We had to reel his acting in. Anyway, it was enough to send those people scurrying away before they even unpacked their tent."

Driverton sure was something else. "That was genius."

"And more effective than any of us thought it would be."

I didn't have the heart to tell him that the full package of how isolated Driverton was, in addition to the unwelcoming attention of an entire community, added to a huge man foaming at the mouth might have worked without mention of the virus. Let him believe it was all Reana.

"The water's warm this time of year. Would you like to swim?"

"Really?"

I took his hand. We made our way down the hill to the base of the waterfall. Carefully, we stepped from rock to rock until we reached a large, flat boulder that the water had chosen to flow around. We sat on the edge of it and removed our shoes. As soon as I dipped my toes beneath the water, I squealed. "You call that warm?"

His smile held boyish charm. "Warm-ish. It *is* mountain-fed." He put an arm around me, and I melted against him.

We sat there, soaking in the sound of the splashing water as well as the feel of each other. "Looks like our friends are getting married," I said softly.

"It sure does." He tucked me closer to his side. "There's something I need to say, but I'm not good at expressing how I feel."

My chest tightened in anticipation. "Just say it and we'll sort it out."

"I'm not ready for you yet."

I let out a breath. "What does that mean?"

He kept his gaze ahead and on the waterfall. "I'm struggling, Megan. I want to be with you, but I don't want to be with *me*. Not the me I currently am. Does that make sense?"

I studied his profile and let his words sink in. He'd said something similar before, but I could now see how deeply he believed it. "I think so."

"I've got some shit to figure out before I can be anything to anyone."

My heart sank. "I understand."

"I don't think you do." He turned to face me. "I don't want to be with anyone but you."

I nodded even though I was thoroughly confused.

He continued, "And I don't want you to be with anyone but me."

I coughed. *"But?"* There was a but. I didn't want to hear it, but I also needed to.

"But not today. Not until I can look myself in the eye and know I'm someone you *should* be with."

I looked away and took a deep breath. "I don't know what you're asking for, Ollie."

"Something that's more than I deserve, but that I need—time."

Part of me wanted to promise him anything and everything he needed, but my pride kicked in. "While I do what? Wait? While you figure things out on your own? That doesn't sound fair." And once again it put what I'd been doing with my weekly friend/dates in a bad light, which made the whole conversation even more uncomfortable.

"You're right. Hang on to Arnie and Bryant until I'm ready."

I turned and shoved myself out of Ollie's embrace. "Now you're being an ass."

He ran a hand down his face and turned away again. "I want to be the man I felt like I was when we rescued Everette and that woman."

My heart ached for him. "You *are* that man."

He shook his head. "Not yet, but at least now I have a goal beyond survival. I want to look myself in the mirror and be proud of the man staring back at me. If I knew what it'd take for that to happen, I'd ask you to come on that journey with me—but all I know is that I have to make some serious changes."

"And I'd be in your way?"

His hand sought mine. "I told you I wouldn't explain this well. I have to do this, Megan. I have to do something. I feel like if I fail at this, I won't be someone anyone will want to be around. I couldn't do that to you."

"Do you think people can only be together during the good times?"

The dark torment in his eyes when he met my gaze again convinced me this wasn't a game to him. He was letting me see past his Gatekeeper to the real him and it was heartbreaking to realize how beaten down he was. "I'm drowning, Megan. And I refuse to take you down with me."

I let out a shaky breath and tightened my hand on his. "I need more than you're offering."

We sat in silence for a long time, simply holding hands while facing the waterfall. "The prince looked ready to offer you more."

I elbowed Ollie in the ribs—hard. "Jerk."

"So, no fairy-tale ending for you?"

With a huff, I said, "I will punt you into the water if you

don't stop."

His laugh echoed against the rocks. "I have something for you."

"You do?" Every time I thought I understood Ollie, he threw me another curveball. "What?"

He shifted so he could reach into the front pocket of his jeans and pulled out a small square box. A ring? Didn't he just say he didn't want to make any promises to me? And wasn't it way too soon? I accepted the box and held it in front of me while a rush of emotions came and went and came again.

"Open it," he murmured.

When I removed the cover, I blinked in surprise. On the black velvet was a small silver turtle. I pulled it out and discovered it was attached to a chain.

"It's just sterling silver, but it reminded me of you."

I turned it over and read what was engraved there. "To my Turtle Lady." Tears filled my eyes because I was and I wasn't.

"If I could afford—"

I laid a finger across his lips. "I love it. Help me put it on." After handing him the necklace, I turned and held my hair up. He reached around my neck and then clasped the chain behind it. While my hair was still up, he bent and kissed the curve of my neck. Nothing had ever felt so right.

I turned slowly and looked into those beautiful eyes of his. "You're not playing fair."

"I'm not playing." He cupped my face between his hands. "I'm heading into battle—with myself. I can't promise I'll come back to you, because if I fail, I won't. And if you decide I'm not worth the wait, I'll use the last of whatever good is left in me to be happy for whoever you do end up with."

Fighting against an urge to hand my heart right over to him, I said, "If you're trying to get me to fuck you again, this isn't working for me."

His head whipped back, and his hands fell from my face. I wasn't proud that I'd caused the hurt darkening his eyes. I opened my mouth to apologize, then snapped it shut again. I needed him to raise some walls between us because mine were crumbling. "That's probably for the best." Our gaze met and locked and just above a whisper, he said, "For now."

"Shelby and Everette are planning a short engagement. I'll probably be around more to help her prepare for it." I turned back toward the waterfall. "Do you want me to stay at a hotel when I come to town?"

"I want you to stay wherever you're most comfortable."

Shaking my head, my hand went to the turtle charm nestled at the top of my cleavage. "I've already been with someone who promised me the world then didn't make me his priority. Been there. Done that. Not looking to take that ride twice."

The silence that followed was heavy, so heavy I considered getting up and heading back to the party.

"I never want that to be our story. I'm sure it's not fair of me to ask but give me time to become someone who won't let you down."

I wiped tears from the corners of my eyes. "Okay."

His arm wrapped around me again and I scooted closer to him, resting my cheek on his shoulder. He kissed the top of my head then turned back to look out over the water.

I sniffed. In an attempt to lighten what was an almost unbearably sad moment, I joked, "Why did you suggest swimming? That water is so cold that if I'd said yes, your dick would have run to hide in your abdomen."

A laugh rumbled out of him. "I love the way you express yourself."

I pinched his side. "I'm right, though."

He took his hand and laid it high on his thigh, just beneath what was a significant bulge in the front of his jeans. "Have you considered that cold water would have helped make this conversation easier to have? It's challenging to tell you I don't want to fuck you when stripping you down and taking you right here on this rock is all I can think about."

I hid a smile as pleasure flooded in. "Oh, so you're suffering a little, are you?"

He kissed the top of my head again. "The right thing to do is to wait, and that's what I intend to do."

There was something incredibly noble about his declaration, so I didn't choose that moment to remind him that we'd already crossed the line he was struggling not to. I touched the turtle charm on my neck again and relaxed against his side, safe in the knowledge that he'd protect me even from himself.

Chapter Eighteen

Ollie

THE NEXT FEW weeks were difficult. Bradford agreed to work with Levi, Katie, and me again, but only after Everette's wedding. Levi and I promised each other we'd give working with Bradford a real shot and that meant sobering up. I stopped drinking, but it wasn't easy.

Megan stayed at my mother's house on the weekends leading up to the wedding, and that also wasn't easy. When hundreds of miles separated us, I called her each night and we talked for hours. It might have been due to how my spare time became filled with pig waste as one side hustle ended and I took on the next, but I kept my distance from her in Driverton.

I danced with Megan at the wedding and it was pure torture. More than once, I asked myself if I was being an idiot. Her face lit up when she saw me. The chemistry between us when we danced was mind-scrambling hot. All I had to do to be in her bed was put aside my fucking pride, but I couldn't.

I wanted better for her.

The night before Levi, Katie, and I were scheduled to start working with Bradford again, I stayed late to close up Little Willie's. My phone notified me of a new email. I shouldn't have read it. It was from the hospital where my father had been treated right before he died. They'd uncovered an outstanding bill for fifty thousand dollars. If I didn't pay it, they threatened to put a lien on the restaurant.

Alone, I laughed until tears filled my eyes then reached for a bottle of whiskey. It took six shots to ease the tension in my chest. It took a few more before I opened my phone, found the email again, and hit delete.

What could they fucking do?

I had nothing for them to take. They'd threatened to force me to sell my assets—like I had any. I considered sending them my pig-shit-stained boots. The more I drank the funnier that idea seemed.

I didn't call Megan that night.

I didn't call anyone.

I drank myself into a stupor and slept in one of the booths. It wasn't the first time, but I'd hoped I'd never go to that place again.

I WOKE UP feeling worse than I smelled. It didn't matter how much soap I used, I couldn't get the scent of pig manure off me or out of my truck. My mood wasn't helped by finding out that Bradford's "training" consisted of digging holes for fence posts around his large farm. Manually. Not because it was the best method or because none of us owned the machinery that could have gotten the job done quickly, but because he wanted to punish us for quitting the first time.

At Bradford's farm, the heated looks Katie and Levi exchanged every time they thought I wasn't looking didn't help my mood. Levi had always been and would always be my best friend, but that didn't mean I wouldn't kill him if he slept with my cousin. For all the good that Levi did and was, I'd never known anyone to go through women faster. Friends don't judge, but friends also keep promises to each other, and Levi had promised to keep his hands off Katie.

I'd like to say I kept my sour mood from spilling over onto those I cared about, but I snapped at both Levi and Katie until Levi pulled me aside to ask if I was okay. I told him I was drinking again but left out the reason that had brought me back to my knees. Maybe it was my pride. Maybe I didn't want to fucking think about it. Either way, Levi did what best friends do—he made me apologize to Katie then convinced Bradford to come up with a cover story while I went to a rehab in Boston.

Not one single part of that day was easy. I hated admitting I needed help. I hated that Bradford was the one who made an offer I couldn't refuse. He was willing not only to send me to Boston to a rehab center, but also to make sure I came back qualified to use and maintain the computer system Clay planned to install in his Driverton underground headquarters.

Most of all, I hated the look in Bradford's eyes when he made the offer. He wasn't doing it for *me*. I wasn't the one he respected. Levi had asked for a favor, and I was the recipient of that request. Nothing more. Nothing less.

It was difficult to be grateful to someone who was clearly disgusted by me. I could have defended myself and my choices, but instead, I looked back at him with just as much disdain.

But I took what he offered because I was sinking fast.

I tried to tell my mother the cover story about how going to Boston was a huge training opportunity, but she saw right through that lie. She knew without asking that I was drinking again. Mothers have a weird sixth sense when it comes to things like that. When I admitted I was going away to sober up, she hugged me and cried. I may have cried a little with her. Never had I felt less worthy of being cared about by anyone.

I EXPECTED BRADFORD to take me to Boston, but Clay and his fucking little dog, Boppy, picked me up the next morning. Unfortunately, I was sober when he told me from that point on he'd be my Fairy Godfather Extraordinaire. I thought he was kidding, but he wasn't.

He flew with me and my slight pig waste smell in one of his expensive helicopters to Boston. I was emotionally shattered by then, completely uncaring of what would come next. So, when he said we needed to spend a full day at a spa, I didn't even ask what that would entail.

Having never been to a spa before, I couldn't say if the one we went to was normal or not. All I know was for what felt like the longest day of my life, Clay, Boppy, and I were soaked, scrubbed, massaged, trimmed, exfoliated, and catered to by so many staff members I stopped trying to remember their names. I was escorted from room to room in nothing more than a big, fluffy white robe and slippers.

When I was finally given the option of changing into clothing again, I was informed that everything I'd brought had mysteriously disappeared. I didn't have enough fight left in me to care. I followed Clay to a large room filled with mirrors and racks of clothing. With a wave of his hand, Clay had the people in there scurrying around me, removing my robe, and taking measurements.

Honestly, it was the fucking weirdest experience of my life. Eventually, someone handed me a pair of underwear and socks. I tried on several casual outfits then a few business suits. All while Clay sat with Boppy and called out instructions.

Decisions were made. Items were sorted while others were ordered. I was standing in the middle of the room in a pair of khakis, a button-down navy shirt, and the most comfortable pair of shoes I'd ever worn when everyone but Clay left the room.

With Boppy tucked under his arm, he walked over to

me. "Now you're ready for rehab."

I laughed even though I didn't find anything about the situation funny. "You didn't have to do this, Clay."

He stepped closer and the emotion in his eyes surprised me. His voice was deeper than usual as well. "Once upon a time, my little brother needed someone, and I wasn't there for him. I failed him when he needed me the most. But Driverton took him in and protected him as I should have. Cooper told me how your family fed him daily at Little Willie's for years. Let me help you, Ollie. Not because you need me to, but because I need to repay some of the kindness you've shown my family."

Rumor was that Clay had more money than God, but I'd been raised too proud to accept charity. "I can't afford to repay you now, but as soon as I can—"

"You have nothing because you've been generous with all you had. Do you expect Cooper to repay you for all the times you fed him?"

"Of course not."

"And I won't accept a penny from you."

"You don't owe us anything, Clay."

"Oh, I do and I'll let you in on a little secret. Over the next month everyone in Driverton will receive notice that the government is making reparations for a land grab they did for the old logging company that came through the area. Some have already been contacted. Some will hear about it soon. Your mother's house is paid off. As is Little Willie's. I did that because I know how good all of you have been to my family. So today? A few outfits? This is nothing."

My jaw dropped. "Clay. No one expects you to pay for anything."

"And they will never know I did it because it's a secret."

Confused, I asked, "Why tell me then?"

He cuddled Boppy to him. "Because I trust you and I want you to have proof that I do. Bradford thinks he knows everything, but he looks at everyone in terms of threat assessment. You and your family were an enigma to me. How can you work so hard and still have nothing? I dug a little and, I hope this doesn't sound weird, but I fell in love."

I grimaced. Did I accidentally end up in some unconventional relationship with Clay? "Clay, I like you, but I don't *like* you."

His eyebrows shot up then he laughed. "Not in love with *you*—in love with the good your family has done. I haven't found a person yet in Driverton who hasn't been helped in some way by you or your family. If that doesn't deserve a Fairy Godfather intervention, I don't know what does."

I took a deep breath and tried to process what he was saying. If he'd really paid off my mother's mortgage as well as Little Willie's, I was a hell of a lot closer to being free than I thought I could get any time soon. Sure, there were still medical bills, but I'd chip away at those with the money I normally put toward the mortgages. A shudder of relief passed through me and I blinked a few times quickly. "I don't know how to thank you, Clay."

"You've already done your part. This is *me* thanking *you*." He gave my shoulder a pat.

"Ready to go check in to your home for the next few weeks?"

I nodded. As we walked out of the spa, Clay motioned for me to stand taller with my shoulders back. "Walk like the man you were born to be."

I took a deep breath, squared my shoulders and straightened my back. My father had been a good, moral man. He'd taught me to be honest, humble, generous, and kind. I can only imagine what my father would have had to say about me working with a Fairy Godfather, but beneath all his money and showboating, Clay didn't seem so different than my father had been. No matter how tough the times, we'd never turned anyone away from Little Willie's. No one who came in feeling alone and hopeless left without the community being called in to rally support.

How was this different?

Clay was one of us now, wasn't he?

The more he helped me, the more I could help others.

My father would have approved of that plan.

Chapter Nineteen

Ollie

THREE WEEKS OF healthy eating, working out, and daily counseling had me feeling like I could start my life fresh. I didn't have to carry the weight of every mistake I'd made or require the approval of all around me. Who I'd been didn't matter as much as who I would become. What people thought about me would never again matter more than what I knew to be true of myself.

Not only were the counselors at the facility helpful, but Andrew Barrington, a friend of Bradford's, visited daily and offered to be my sponsor. He said I could call him, day or night, if I felt myself wavering. He was also an alcoholic, but it had been years since he'd touched a drop of liquor. When he offered to show me how running and sparring daily could replace my addiction, I took him up on it. He'd worked out with me every single day and I was more grateful than I knew how to express.

It was my last day at the facility, and I was feeling better than I had in . . . maybe ever. I was waiting in my room, my things packed and ready to go.

The door opened and a woman with gentle features and graying hair entered. She was too well dressed to work at the center. I wasn't one who believed in auras or things like that, but when she smiled at me it felt as if she'd hugged me. "Hello, Oliver, my name is Sophie Barrington."

Barrington. *This must be Andrew's mother. Odd time for a visit, but I guess meeting me on the last day is a better choice than on my first.* I stood and walked over to greet her. "Nice to meet you, Mrs. Barrington. Most people call me Ollie."

"I'll call you whatever you'd like me to, but Oliver is a beautiful name."

I nodded. "It was my father's middle name. He's the only one who called me by it."

"So, Ollie?"

My nickname sounded odd coming from a woman who held herself with such quiet grace. I dipped my head, "Oliver is fine."

Her smile reminded me of the one my mother used to give me when I was much younger and had done something to please her. "My son Andrew speaks highly of you."

"I didn't know if I'd see him today, so I didn't say everything to him I should have, but what he did for me . . . not only did it work . . . but if he ever needs anything from me, I owe him so much. I know he came because Bradford asked him to, but it still means a lot."

"Bradford did ask my son Ian to check in on you, but

Clay is the reason Andrew flew up from Florida to help you."

"I don't understand."

"Clay told me you're a remarkable young man with the kind of integrity my family values in the people we welcome into our lives. Of course, I wasn't allowed to meet you until you were thoroughly vetted by my overprotective sons, but Andrew endorsed you, so here I am."

It was difficult to look her in the eye, but I could hear Clay's voice in my head telling me to hold myself to the standard of the man I wanted to be, so I kept my gaze steady. "You're kindly overlooking where we are."

Mrs. Barrington looked around. "Oliver, if we were all measured by our lowest moments, I wouldn't be allowed near my children or grandchildren. I've spent time in facilities not too different than this one, I don't consider myself lesser for it."

I didn't know what to say to that.

Her expression was filled with compassion. "It feels like a lifetime ago, but my son Kade was taken from us and the loss of him shattered me to my core. He's back in our lives now and I could be angry at the time I missed, but I choose to be grateful to those who saved him instead. Losing him changed me. Humbled me. Tested me in ways that nearly broke me irreparably. But I made it through and I'm stronger for it. You'll make it through this, Oliver. I believe that."

I let out a slow, emotionally charged breath. "I hope I can one day speak of this time in my life like that."

"You will." Her smile returned. "Clay would have picked you up today, but I asked him to allow me."

My shoulders rose in question. "Why?"

"I wanted the honor of meeting one of the men who cared for Clay's brother." Her hand went to her chest. "When Clay shared what your family did for him... I understood why Driverton and all of you are so important to him. The people who hid my son to protect him, the ones who filled his life with love and laughter when I wasn't there to, in my heart they are family. Nothing I could ever do would feel like enough. Clay is like one of my sons. If you're family to Clay, you're family to me. You'll be staying with him, but I'd also like to play a part in your journey to success."

"I mean no offense when I say this, but Clay has already been more generous than I'm comfortable with. Knowing there are people out there who want to see me win is enough of a role in my journey."

She took a moment to consider my words before asking, "How would you define success? What are you looking for, for yourself?"

Her question rocked through me, and I struggled at first to articulate my goal. Then the answer came to me, crisp and clear. "I want to be the man my father asked me to be. I'm trying, but it's so fucking hard." I apologized for swearing as soon as it registered to me that I had.

She touched my arm gently. "I don't know what your

father asked of you, but I am a parent, and I know he wouldn't have expected you to get there on your own. I've felt lost and alone, even with my family gathered around. We all did. Instead of letting each other in and asking for help when we needed it, our family hid our weaknesses from each other and paid a hefty price for it. I don't hide my mistakes anymore. I don't second-guess my instincts. And I don't turn down help when it's offered."

I nodded. "I understand, but I was raised to earn my own way."

Her hand tightened on my arm. "My husband is a proud man, just like you. And, Lord, my sons take after him. I won't offer you financial support, but I would like you to dine with us on a regular basis while you're in Boston. Each of my children are gifted in different ways and they're all in a place where they'd happily pay forward some of the good that has come to them. Asher can show you how to outsmart the devil himself in the boardroom. Grant will have you designing a financial plan for the next five generations of your family. Ian's my diplomat. If you want to know how to diffuse a situation, he's your man. Kade owns a helicopter tour business and has just opened a flight school. Lance is an architect. He'll talk your ear off about what that's like as a career if you let him. My daughter, Kenzi, is quite the public speaker now. You could learn a lot from her as well. And don't even get me started on how talented their spouses are."

It was impossible to wrap my mind around so many

people wanting to help me. "I couldn't ask them—"

"You don't have to. I already did and they've not only agreed but have come up with a schedule of when each of them could work with you. All you have to do is say yes. They won't give you anything but their time. I promise. But what they'll teach you should give you the skills to go off and do some amazing things on your own."

"You're serious? This is real?"

"It's as real as you let it be."

I ran a shaking hand down my face. Things like this didn't happen to people. Not to people like me or anyone I knew.

If things seem too good to be true . . .

Still, I couldn't imagine Mrs. Barrington as anything but an angel. "Thank you."

She nodded toward my bag. "If you're ready, I'll take you to Clay's house."

Something held me back. *Megan.* "Do you mind if I make a quick phone call before we go?"

"Your mother?"

My face flushed. "No."

"Ah, of course." Her smile was amused but understanding. "I'll have my driver pull around to the entrance and meet you there."

"Thank you . . . for everything, Mrs. Barrington."

"Sophie. Call me Sophie. And you're very welcome, Oliver. I'll see you downstairs."

As soon as she'd gone, I took out my phone. I hadn't called Megan since before I'd fallen off the wagon that night at Little Willie's. Would she even take a call from me?

I sent her a text. **You there?**

Nothing.

I called her and when she didn't pick up, I left this message on her voicemail:

> **It's been so long. I understand why you might not want to talk to me, but not a day goes by that I don't think about you. I just finished three weeks of rehab and have a long way to go, but things are turning around. I hope you're doing well.**

After sending it, I stuffed my phone into the pocket of my trousers and headed downstairs to begin phase two of what Clay called my life reboot. I'd grown up with a serious lack of appreciation for those born outside of Driverton, but I was learning that kindness and generosity didn't stop at our town's border.

Chapter Twenty

Megan

AT MY CUBICLE desk at work, I listened to Ollie's message twice before calling Shelby and playing it for her. "Rehab?" I asked her. "So he didn't go to Boston to take computer classes. That was a lie."

"That he told you the truth now is huge," Shelby said gently.

"He could have told me before he left. Or told me anything instead of ghosting me. I spent weeks thinking he didn't care enough to tell me he was leaving and wondering why being in Boston meant he no longer had the time for me."

"I'm sorry."

"If I meant anything to him, he wouldn't have put me through that."

"Or he was ashamed he couldn't stop drinking on his own and needed help. Didn't he ask you to give him time to become someone who wouldn't disappoint you?"

"That was before he started calling me every night. I thought we were building a friendship if not something significantly more."

"Not sure if this helps, but Everette has never seen Ollie act like this with anyone. He thinks Ollie doesn't want to be with you until he has himself figured out. Everette also thinks it would be better for both of you if you gave Ollie the time he asked for."

"Well, Levi didn't impulsively have sex with him and then start having feelings for him because of it, did he?" When Shelby didn't give any sign that she was stunned by that admission, I said, "You knew."

"I guessed. I mean, your complete lack of interest in a prince who wanted to shower you with gifts was a pretty clear giveaway."

I waved a hand through the air. "See, that's a sign that Ollie isn't good for me. I passed up a perfectly good chance to relocate and help rule a foreign country I've never heard of . . . Okay, that doesn't sound like something I would have wanted to do even before I met Ollie, but I didn't even give it a chance."

"You're upset about more than the prince. Talk to me."

"Do you remember Bryant?"

"The widower you see every Friday?"

"Not anymore. I introduced him to someone from my office and they seem meant for each other. He's happier than I've ever seen him."

"How do you feel about that?"

"Surprisingly good. He thanked me for being someone he could talk to when he needed that more than he needed a relationship. He credited my friendship with why he made it past the worst of his grief. I felt guilty after Cole said he and I had been holding each other in limbo, but that's not how Bryant saw it. He needed time to heal, and I gave that to him."

"Was Ollie the reason you called it off with Cole?"

"Yes and no. Meeting Ollie made me realize there was no real spark between the men I was seeing and me. Cole started me thinking about how what I was doing might not be healthy for either side. It was a relief to hear Bryant say it hadn't been a waste of time for him. We were helping each other."

"How was he helping you?"

I didn't have a clear answer to that yet, so I pivoted. "I'm also no longer seeing Arnie."

"The bodybuilder?"

"Yes."

"You okay with that?"

"I am. We didn't have anything in common outside of liking to eat out. It was easy to break off and, honestly, I doubt he misses me. We were more of a habit than a relationship."

"I didn't ask how he felt. You went from having something to do every night of the week to . . . what?"

"I'm still figuring that out."

"Okay, I have a question. Are you looking for me to listen and commiserate or would you like some advice?"

I sighed. "A little of both."

"That's fair," she said, sounding slightly amused. "Back to Ollie's message. It obviously upset you."

"It did. I was beginning to think I meant something to him. When he left without saying anything to me, I made myself okay with not meaning anything to him." My hand went protectively to the turtle necklace I hadn't taken off since Ollie had given it to me. "Well, mostly okay."

"You were never okay with it."

"Yeah."

"So, you're finding all of this confusing."

"Very much so."

"Are you ready to hear what I think?"

The phone on my desk rang. I sent it to voicemail. "No, but I want to anyway."

"I think you focus so much energy on how others feel that you've lost touch with your own needs."

That wasn't at all what I thought she'd say. I half expected her to validate my fear that I'd selfishly wasted the time of five good men for no other reason than I didn't like to be alone.

She continued, "You haven't been yourself since my parents were murdered. Until recently I was struggling with my own grief so much, I didn't think about how it might have affected you. You never had a problem being alone before they died."

"I had you."

"We had each other. But, even then, we weren't together every day. You used to sign up for cooking classes and those craft classes, remember?"

It was true, but it still felt like someone else's life. "Some of that pottery made good Christmas presents."

"It did. I also remember marveling that you would go to a movie solo if everyone else was busy."

"I don't know how I ever did that."

"You explored Driverton by yourself. How is that different?"

"That's completely different. Driverton feels so—" I choked back the word at the tip of my tongue: *safe*.

"I get it. Everette bought Tyr for me because I was struggling to sleep on my own. I don't like to talk about how much last year changed me, but I'm beginning to understand that the things I deny are the things I give power to. I can finally, without shame, admit that losing my parents the way I did left me feeling vulnerable and afraid. That's why I moved in with Jeff. He made me feel safe. I didn't love him, and I ended up being a poor choice for him, but he was what I needed in the beginning. Someone murdered my parents, Megan. It would be weird if that didn't make me a different person. It affected you too. They were a part of your life. You loved them."

"I did."

"And how we lost them was horrific. It changed how safe I feel even in my own home."

I breathed in and let my walls down. "Me too."

"When I was lost, you lent me your strength and I needed it. I don't know what I would have done without you."

My eyes misted over. "I've often felt that way about you."

"So, when I say this, I want you to hear the love in my words. You can't fix Ollie. He doesn't even want you to. He's fighting a different demon than we're fighting, but one that he needs to conquer just as much."

"I understand that. When I force myself to be logical about this, I respect him for getting help."

"I'm not him, so I can't speak for how he feels, but when I was in the thick of my battle, I didn't have the bandwidth for Everette. He was so good to me, but I wasn't in a place where I could receive that yet."

"I remember."

"He gave me the time I needed."

"So, you're saying I should wait this out with Ollie? Put my life on hold while he figures his shit out?"

"No, I'm saying you can live your life while leaving the door to your heart open to him. What do *you* need?"

Another work call came through and I sent it to voicemail. "I don't know. I thought I was doing fine, but I was really filling my time with distractions."

"Okay, let's try this. Tell me five things that make you happy."

"You."

"Same. That's one."

I touched the turtle on my necklace. "When I'm actually with Ollie it's amazing. It's not just flutters and heat. I feel connected to him."

"That's two."

"This is going to sound corny, but I have so much fun with his mother. We cook, laugh, swap stories. I wish I could do that with my own mother."

"Three."

"I enjoy being part of a community. In my building, I can go weeks without having a conversation with anyone. My office is the same. The customer service department sucks and although I've lasted, the turnover rate is high. My favorite part of the job is how much vacation time I've accrued."

"So four, you enjoy interacting with people."

"Yes."

"One more."

"Do I sound pathetic if I say I love Myrtle? I know she's not soft and fluffy, but when I put her on a little skateboard, she follows me around my apartment and zooms. She makes me laugh and that always lifts my mood."

There was a smile in her voice. "Your list doesn't require anyone's approval. This is about figuring out what you want and taking action on the parts of the list you have control over. You can't make Ollie be ready to be with you, but you can fill your life with things that make you happy so you're either in a better place when he does come to you—or you've filled your life with enough things that make you happy that it's okay if he doesn't."

"When did you become so wise?"

"You know how they say what doesn't kill you makes you stronger? I didn't believe that a year ago, but I get it now. When Everette went missing, I knew I could find him and that no one could stop me from going to him. That's a level of confidence I didn't have before losing my parents. So, yeah, I'm scarred from that experience, but damn, those scars have made me stronger."

"And you think I'll discover the same about myself?"

"I know you will, as soon as you stop trying to convince yourself you're the same person you've always been and start following your happiness."

I nodded as I thought through what she was saying. "I hate this job. It's sucking the life out of me."

"So, find a different one."

"There's not a lot of opportunity in Driverton, but I'd like to live closer to you. Maybe I could get a job in a town close enough to see you more often."

"I'd love that. Mrs. Williams would love to see more of you too."

"Is it wrong to stay at Ollie's house while he and I . . ."

"You could always ask him if it bothers him, but I don't think it does."

Even though she hadn't asked for it, I added, "I want to be outside more. I go from my shoebox of an apartment to this gray cubicle. It's against office policy to put anything up on the walls. Sometimes I wonder if I'll enjoy being in my coffin more than being here."

Shelby laughed at that. "That's a clear sign that it's time to make a change. When would you like help moving? Tonight? Two weeks from now?"

"I have six months left on my apartment lease."

"Do you want to stay there that long?"

"No. No, I don't."

"Then let's find a way to get you that money. When we put our heads together there's nothing we can't do. Sometimes, if you find a replacement tenant, they'll forgive what you owe. Let's start there."

Hope surged in me. "You make it sound so easy."

"It is once you stop asking yourself *if* you can, and start asking *how* you can."

"Did you get that from Everette?"

"I did and he got it from Bradford. All I'm doing is paying that wisdom forward."

"Well, I like it. Okay, I'm doing it. I'll give my two weeks' notice today."

A female voice boomed behind me. "Is that a personal call? End it now. Unless you don't want to work here anymore." Threatening to fire someone was my boss's preferred go-to. She didn't ask if there was an issue or pretend to care about anyone's life outside the office. I wondered if she knew how often it was that attitude that played into why people didn't stay.

Suddenly giddy, I said, "I'll talk to you later, Shelby." After ending the call, I turned my chair and rose to my feet. "About that last part . . ."

Chapter Twenty-One

Ollie

THE LONGER I stayed in Boston, the more surreal it felt. Clay credited my good manners and general humility as the reason Sophie Barrington decided to "take me under her wing." I didn't deserve the amount of faith she instantly had in me, but I will say that her opinion of me became more important than my own mother's.

I'm not entirely sure why.

I suspect part of it was because she represented a fresh start. There was no disappointment in her eyes. When she said she saw real potential in me and she'd help me develop it, I believed her.

What I quickly learned was that Sophie didn't say anything she didn't mean. As the matriarch of the Barrington family, she assembled an uncomfortable amount of support for me. For weeks, every waking hour of my day was filled with meetings with one or more members of her family. From them, I learned how to navigate through the world of the wealthy. They instructed me on attire, social etiquette, and the fine art of saying less when in a situation I wasn't familiar with. The initial challenge I faced was not to be offended when they modeled how to greet and speak to certain people. It wasn't until I noticed that even the Barringtons adjusted their behavior and speech when dealing with powerful people that I understood they weren't judging me, but rather giving me the key to gain access.

Soon, it didn't matter that my bank account was nearly empty. I was beginning to understand how to walk into a room with the confidence to put those who didn't know me quickly at ease. The trick was to not see myself as a stray cat walking into a den of lions, but as a fellow lion. When I struggled with that idea at first, Sophie's husband, Dale, took me aside and assured me that most of the people I met were as in debt as they were rich. The world of the wealthy was a game in which money was an imaginary currency frequently traded by people who pretended to know what they were doing. What held value in any circle was knowledge, because that's where true power resided.

With that in mind, the Barringtons set out to educate me. Yes, I took classes in cyber security and coding, but I also learned secrets to maintaining generational wealth, how to win a negotiation, the art of recognizing a good contract, and all about taxes. They also schooled me on flying helicopters, sharpshooting, and combat techniques.

I was seated at my desk at one of Asher Barrington's

business sites when he appeared at the door of my office. For the past two weeks, he'd allowed me to shadow him during certain hours of the day. When I'd asked him if I needed to sign an NDA, he'd laughed and said if I shared anything I overheard with anyone, he'd make sure it was the last thing I was capable of sharing.

There was a reason Asher Barrington was called "The Hammer" even by those who liked him. Rumor was he'd mellowed after marrying and having children—but not that much. "I'm heading out. What are you working on?"

I held my tablet up for him to see. "Just processing today's meetings. Summarizing your negotiation techniques."

He leaned against the doorframe and smiled. "Good. This is the stuff no one learns in college."

I replaced the tablet on my desk and stood. "I can tell why you're successful."

"You can?"

"You start with statistics, charm, and your competitor's weaknesses then steamroll through obstacles, and by the time you're done, they feel they won't succeed without you."

"Thank you, but there's something you're missing. Win enough and people will anticipate losing to you." He tapped his temple. "Success and failure start here. Often, the outcome of a negotiation is determined before either side speaks."

"So, it's an attitude more than a skill?"

"No, it's skill and experience that breed confidence.

Right now, you're watching and learning. You won't know what I'm talking about until you're tested. You'll lose more than you win at first, but when you find your strength, you'll know it . . . everyone will."

"Thank you for taking the time to explain this to me."

He folded his arms across his chest. "I have a question for you. If I had a magic wand and could give you one thing—anything, what would it be?"

"Like a Fairy Godfather?" I smirked because Clay's practice of calling himself a Fairy Godfather didn't mesh well with Asher's no-nonsense personality.

"Fuck you," he responded with a laugh. "I'm serious. What are you doing all of this for?"

"Your mother asked me that too. My answer hasn't changed. I want to be the man my father asked me to be."

"Why?"

"What do you mean why?"

"Why does that matter to you?"

"Because he was a good man."

"And you want to be like him?"

"Yes and no. He gave away everything he had. More than everything. He left my mother and me with what felt like an insurmountable debt. I refuse to put anyone I care about in that situation. I want to learn how to make enough money to be generous but not to the detriment of my family."

"What would you do with a million dollars?"

"Now? I'd invest it in something that made income over

time without diminishing the original amount."

"No flashy car? No dream vacations?"

I shrugged. "There's only one place I'd like to go, but I'm not allowing myself that trip yet."

He arched an eyebrow.

I didn't say Megan's name, but I didn't have to. Asher hadn't gotten where he was and stayed there as long as he had without knowing everything there was to know about those he dealt with.

"Ah. Yes. What's your plan with that?"

"I don't have one yet." I exhaled audibly.

"Then you'll fail, both yourself and her."

Ouch. "Wow, curb your optimism."

He held my gaze. "Are you under some kind of misconception that I care how you feel? Both my mother and Clay asked me to teach you what you need to know to be successful. Here's another trade secret: Very few people care how you feel about anything. I ask questions because I want to know who I'm dealing with and to assess your potential. Period."

"And you've already determined I'll fail?"

"No, *you* have. You want to be successful? Make it happen. You want Megan in your life? Take measurable action toward that goal. Next time we talk, don't waste my time telling me what you *want*. Tell me how *you'll get it*." Asher pushed off the wall and walked away.

I went to the window of the small office and looked at all

the expensive cars in the lot below. How would Asher have responded had I told him his advice wasn't that much different from what my favorite counselor had doled out at the rehab center? Neither sugar-coated their advice, and both held me accountable for shaping my outcome by shaping my thoughts.

My phone buzzed with a call from Levi. Although we'd talked several times while I was in rehab, our last conversation had been strained, and I didn't want to dig into why. Opportunities like I was being offered came around once in a person's life, if they came at all. I didn't answer because I wasn't ready. Once I found my footing, I'd call him, and he'd understand. To maintain momentum, I couldn't go back to Driverton, not even mentally.

But I could take measurable action in another area. With a swipe, I found Megan's number and called her. This time she answered. "Hi."

God, her voice was everything I'd remembered it being. Sweet. Tempting. Sexy as hell. I wished we hadn't met yet and that she would only know the me I was becoming.

What would Asher do in my place? He'd be direct. Bold. He'd have a plan. Since I was no longer paying two mortgages, I still had the money from my last side job. "What are you doing this weekend?" Weekends in Boston were quiet. The Barringtons tended to gather with their spouses and children. I usually spent that time with Clay. Sometimes we traveled. Sometimes he dragged me to museums. This weekend he was planning to go away with his wife which meant I was free.

"Packing."

Wait? What? "Where are you going?"

"Don't laugh."

"I'd never."

"I quit my job and I'm taking a lesser paying position at a turtle sanctuary about an hour from Driverton so I can see Shelby more often. Also, turtle conservation is something I feel passionate about."

"That's my Turtle Lady." Even though she couldn't see it, a huge smile spread across my face.

Breathlessly, she said, "I'm excited. The sanctuary takes in injured and unwanted turtles. They've been looking for someone who can run an educational outreach program—both for new owners as well as the general public. Myrtle and I are going to advocate for turtles both in homes as well as in the wild. I hope Myrtle stays humble after she becomes social media famous."

"When do you move?"

"Monday. I rented a moving container and will be spending all weekend filling it."

"Would you like help?" She didn't say anything for long enough that I was sure she was trying to come up with a way to say she had more than enough help. For all I knew she had men who were only in her life to box things.

"For a few hours or for . . . longer?"

The way she asked the question sent my blood rushing away from my brain. I did my best to sound unaffected by the possibilities of what *longer* might entail. "I'd need to be back in Boston on Monday morning."

"So, you'd stay . . . here?"

"Or I can get a hotel room. Whatever you're comfortable with. I've missed you." There, *that* was honest, clear, and bold.

After another long pause, she said, "I've missed you too." She groaned. "I do want to see you. I'd love the help. Can we decide everything else later?"

"Absolutely."

"Okay, then, yes. I'll send you my current address."

Chapter Twenty-Two

Megan

"WE'RE NOT GOING to have sex," I blurted to a stunned, even better looking than I remembered Ollie who was standing at my door with a bouquet of forget-me-nots.

He tipped his head to one side, gave his jaw a scratch, then shot me a grin that warmed me right down to my toes. "But can I still come in?"

I couldn't have felt more ridiculous. My heart was pounding crazily in my chest and my hands were shaking. I'd told Shelby and Everette not to come that weekend to help me, but I was wondering if it would have been better if they were there. "I should have been clear about that before you drove all the way here."

He held the bouquet out to me. "I still would have come."

I didn't reach for it. Oh, Lord, I'd forgotten how good it felt simply to be this close to him. My whole body came alive beneath his gaze. "I'm serious," I said weakly.

He stepped through the door, closing it behind him. His confidence took my breath away even as it surprised me. He placed the bouquet on the table near the door and said, "Come here."

I stepped right into his embrace, even as I warned myself I shouldn't. Shaking with a tsunami of emotions, I kept my gaze glued to his collarbone. It wasn't him I feared, but the intensity of my response to him. His arms tightened around me, settling me against his chest and tucking me beneath his chin.

His voice was deep and strong. "You're safe with me, Megan. Always."

"I know," I murmured.

"It feels so fucking good to hold you."

I chuckled nervously and relaxed against him. "Yes."

We stood there, just holding each other, for what felt like a blissful eternity. Eventually, he kissed my forehead then touched the turtle charm. "You're still wearing it."

I blushed then met his gaze. "I kind of like the guy who gave it to me."

"Kind of?" His laugh was deep and sexy. "Looks like I'll have to up my game."

Why had I told him nothing would happen between us when this was what I'd been craving? Confused, I stepped back, hoping my brain would start working again if I put some distance between us. As I fought to compose myself, I looked him over. He was dressed casually in jeans and a T-shirt, but not the worn and stained kind I was used to seeing him in. Gone were the running shoes. In their place were brown leather ones. Expensive. His black T-shirt looked new as well. He still had a beard, but it was trimmed short and gave him a slightly edgy but clean-cut appearance.

Beyond the clothing, he had a vitality that hadn't been there before. He filled out his clothing differently—standing straighter, taller, stronger. There was even a visible change in those beautiful eyes. He didn't look down or away. The pain and confusion I'd sensed in him might still be there, but they'd taken the backseat to confidence and humor.

Was this really Ollie?

I brought my hand up to the ponytail I'd chosen out of practicality. Was he disappointed that while he'd been changing, I'd stayed remarkably the same? Mouth dry, I said, "You look different."

"I feel different," he said easily. "Better. Much better."

"I'm glad."

He gave me a slow once-over. "How do you get more beautiful every time I see you?"

I rolled my eyes. "You've obviously been working out. I haven't changed at all."

"There's nothing *to* change. You're gorgeous."

The heat in his gaze supported his claim. I blushed again. "Stop looking at me like that."

"Like what?"

I swallowed hard. "Like I matter to you."

"You do."

Chest tight, I told myself not to say it, but I couldn't help myself. "I was hurt when you left for Boston without telling me."

He rocked back on his heels and hooked his thumbs in his front pockets. "I know."

"We were talking almost every day. I thought—I thought—"

"I'm sorry."

"Part of me understands. It couldn't have been easy for you and I get that, but I . . . I guess I wanted to be someone you could tell the truth to."

All humor was gone from his eyes. He inhaled deeply and took a moment. "I didn't want you to see that side of me."

Emotion blurred my vision. "I wouldn't have judged you. I would have been proud that you were getting help."

He ran his hands down his face. "But *I* wasn't proud of who I was."

I nodded. "I think I understand. I've been making some changes in my own life I'm not telling many people about."

"Really?"

"I'm not saying that so you'll think I'm holding something back. I'm just saying I understand how it might not be easy to share when you're making some changes."

His eyes narrowed. "What kind of changes are you making?"

I picked up the bouquet and invited him to follow me to my kitchen. "These are lovely. Could you help me get the vase from the cabinet? It has to come down anyway."

He opened the cabinet above the stove and retrieved a blue vase but didn't immediately hand it to me. "Talk, Turtle Lady."

I removed the wrapping from the flowers over the sink. "Or what? Will you hold the vase hostage?"

He put it down then moved closer, resting his hip against the counter. "Tell me."

"I would if it were important, but it isn't."

Leaning toward me, he pushed the hair from my ponytail aside and trailed his lips down the curve of my neck.

I shuddered as a wave of excitement zinged through me. *We are not having sex. We are not having sex. We—*

"Please." The heat of his breath on the side of my neck was my undoing. I turned toward him and ran my hands up that broad chest of his.

"You're fighting dirty."

The smile returned to his eyes. "Fighting is not what I want to do with you."

My body jerked and tightened. "If you keep looking at me like that, we won't get much packing done."

He ran his fingers lightly down my back, stopping just above the waistband of my jeans. "That sounds more like a promise than a threat."

It was impossible to pull my gaze from his beautiful eyes.

"There's so much we don't know about each other. So much we should talk out before . . ."

"I'm listening." His hand slid beneath the back of my jeans and my underwear. "And I can stop if this makes it difficult for you to concentrate."

I shifted to allow him better access, loving how his hand slid down to cup one of my ass cheeks. "Everything about you makes it difficult to concentrate."

"Good," he said, then kissed me. One touch led to another, and another, and time suspended as we visited heaven together again.

LATER, TUCKED AGAINST Ollie's side on my couch, I breathed him in and savored the overall sense of peace that being so close to him brought. He kissed the top of my head while tracing the curve of my spine gently. My heartbeat slowed as his did.

"Megan?"

"Mmm?"

"Do you have a bedroom?"

"Of course I do."

"A roommate?"

"No."

"Is your bed already broken down for the move?"

"No." I raised my head reluctantly, not wanting to lessen the wonder of the moment. "Why?"

The expression in his eyes was difficult to discern. "Although having the couch already made up with a pillow and blanket was convenient... Do you sleep out here normally?"

I lowered my head back to his shoulder. "You've never slept on a couch?"

"Of course I have, but I have a feeling you have a reason you choose the couch over your bed."

That wasn't surprising. Despite how much Ollie and I didn't know about each other, when we were together I sensed things about him in a way I only did with Shelby. It was how I'd known he wasn't slacking off when he wasn't at Little Willie's. Running a hand over his chest, I took my time answering. "I sleep better here."

"Because?"

With him it didn't feel necessary to pretend I wasn't damaged. "The cushions against my back make it feel like I'm not alone."

He turned and pulled me closer to him until we were bare chest to bare chest. "Have you always been like that?"

I met his gaze. "No. Only since what happened to Shelby's parents."

His eyes darkened. "That's why you fill your week with dates."

"Filled. I've cleared my calendar."

"For me?" His nostrils flared.

"For *me*."

"Because you're moving?"

"Because I don't need them anymore. Once I understood the role they were playing in my life, I saw that although they made me feel safe in the beginning, they'd begun to hold me back. I was surviving instead of thriving. That's what this move is about. I'm following my joy."

He nodded slowly. "Me too." His eyes darkened. "Funny how that's drawing you closer to Driverton while everything good that's happening for me is drawing me away."

There was nothing remotely funny about that to me. "Everything?" I shouldn't have said it aloud.

He rolled onto his back, still holding me close. "No, not everything."

I could have pushed him for more, but I knew he didn't have the answers. Neither of us did—not yet, anyway. I could be angry with him for not being ready for me, but I wasn't ready for him either.

My racing thoughts slowed, lulled by the rhythmic beat of his heart. In the safety of his arms, I fell asleep.

Chapter Twenty-Three

Ollie

I WOKE BEFORE Megan and slid out from behind her, careful not to rouse her. After retrieving my overnight bag from my rental car, I took a quick shower, got dressed, then headed into her small kitchen. One side of it was filled with unassembled cardboard boxes and packing materials. The other revealed that she hadn't started the packing process yet, at least not in this room.

It wasn't difficult to locate the basics for breakfast, so I made a pot of coffee and cut some fruit. With her hair sticking out in all directions, she appeared in the doorway, gloriously naked. "You're making breakfast?"

There isn't a man on the planet who would have been able to resist her. I didn't even try. Striding across the kitchen, I gathered her to me and gave her a long, lingering kiss before answering, "I am as soon as you tell me what you like."

The heat in her gaze and the smile on her lips told me

her thoughts had quickly gone to where my own had. "Pancakes," she said huskily. "I love blueberry pancakes."

I settled my hands possessively on her rounded backside. "Then that's what you'll get. Now go sit your pretty ass down and I'll bring it to you."

She glanced down at herself. "I should probably go put something on."

"Don't you dare," I growled, then just to see if I could get her to laugh, I added, "But, maybe brush your hair."

I loved the way her breasts jiggled against my chest as her hands flew to her wayward locks. "Is it that bad?"

The next kiss I gave her left her with no doubt about how little her hairstyle mattered. Her arms looped around my neck as she went onto her tiptoes and matched my passion hungrily. When I raised my head, I murmured, "No, it's that good."

Breakfast would have to wait. I swung her up into my arms and carried her to her bedroom.

IT WAS MID-MORNING by the time we surfaced and decided to give breakfast together a second try. I headed back to the kitchen while she showered. When she joined me, dressed in shorts and a T-shirt, I loved her shy smile as she approached the table. "You made pancakes."

I held out the chair for her as she sat, then nuzzled her neck before answering. "Isn't that what you said you wanted?"

She watched me closely as I poured coffee then took the seat across from her. "Thank you." After a few bites, she smiled. "This is delicious."

"Hard to mess up a pancake."

"Although I agree, what's the additional taste to it?"

"Oh, I added some of the yogurt you had in your fridge."

Her smile widened. "Yes, they're sweeter than normal and fluffy. Never thought of using yogurt. I will from now on."

I could have sat there all day basking in the beauty of her. Okay, so she didn't fit the stereotype the media pushed as representative of what men preferred, but she was definitely my type. Everything about her was soft, warm, and inviting. Although she'd chosen a job in customer service, it wasn't surprising to me that following her joy led her to a more nurturing role. "Tell me more about this turtle sanctuary."

Her eyes flashed with excitement as she told me how she'd found it by chance and what a thrill it had been to be offered a position there. "Would you like to meet Myrtle?"

"Sure."

She stepped away and returned with a turtle the size of a cellphone in one hand and a small skateboard in the other. When she put the turtle on the skateboard, it began to zoom around the room and I laughed out loud.

"Myrtle likes to meet people on her own terms. She'll circle you a few times then come over to check you out."

That was exactly what Myrtle did.

Getting to know me involved testing the solidity of my shoe by butting it with her head.

"Does she like to be petted?" I asked, bending to inspect the little creature.

"I wouldn't touch her while you're eating." Myrtle rolled away to her food dish.

Megan washed her hands. "I wasn't sure what a person did with a turtle, but she's hilarious. I didn't set out to get a turtle. When I moved in, the family who'd lived in the apartment before me put Myrtle in a box in the hallway with a sign that she was free. Turtles are one of the most frequently abandoned but most unmentioned pets. They're small and unfortunately some people see them as disposable. She was actually lucky her prior owners went to the trouble of making any attempt at all to rehome her. Many are simply released outside, which is often a death sentence because they're not suited to that environment, or they become invasive species that negatively impact the environment. Her species is from Asia."

"I can't say that is something I've ever really thought about before."

"Exactly. There's a lot people should learn about turtles before they get one. They live longer than people anticipate they will. She could live up to twenty years, but some turtles can live to a hundred. So, if you buy one as a pet for your child, you should really ask yourself if their children or grandchildren will want it as well. People often don't know that all turtles carry Salmonella. That's not a problem if you wash your hands after handling them and clean up after them, but again, that doesn't make it an ideal pet for children—and that's who many people buy them for. Don't even get me started about habitats. A solitary turtle put in a tank with little to no interaction is cruel. They're living creatures. Whenever possible, I get Myrtle outside and in the grass. It's not ideal, but it's the best I can do for her now. If the sanctuary has a habitat she'd be happier in . . . she may end up there. Not because I don't love her. . ."

"But because you do."

Her eyes were shining when her gaze met mine. "Sorry, I don't normally talk so much about Myrtle or get so emotional when I do. Quick, tell me something about yourself before I start to overthink how much I'm sharing."

I brought one of her hands up to my mouth and kissed her knuckles. "What do you want to know?" During our long phone calls, I'd told her all about my friends and family back in Driverton. "I'm not sitting on any secrets."

"I want to hear about Boston."

I gave her an overview of my schedule as well as the list of the many things I was learning. Not used to talking so much about myself, I stopped abruptly. "It's been good."

Her smile was warm. "Sounds amazing. Can you actually fly a helicopter now?"

"Not alone. I need more hours both on the ground and

in the air before I can take my check ride and get certified. Kade Barrington runs an international flight school and seems keen to ensure I qualify. Although, I suspect it's because his mother asked him to."

"Sophie Barrington."

"Yes. Clay asked her to help me and let's just say she took that request seriously. I don't let myself think about it often because I have no idea how I'll ever repay them for this kindness. It's more than a little overwhelming."

Her fingers laced with mine. "From what you've told me, that's how Clay feels toward everyone who helped Cooper. So, maybe they're all just paying kindness forward the way you and your family have always done."

Tipping my head to the side, I let myself get lost in her eyes. God, I wanted to be the man she saw in me. "Imagine the good I'll be able to do once I'm successful."

"I can't wait to see it."

My chest puffed in response to her faith in me. There was a lot I wanted to say, but not yet. Instead, I looked around and asked, "Have you packed anything yet?"

Smiling, she wagged a finger at me. "Don't you worry, I don't have that much stuff."

Laughing, "Not worried, just estimating how much has to be done."

She sat back and sighed. "A lot. I've been patching the wall in the hall outside my bedroom."

"Patching?" I hadn't seen anything when I'd carried her

through that area, but my attention had been fully on her.

"Show me."

"Hang on, I'll put Myrtle away first."

She was back a moment later, waving for me to follow her. The hallway outside her room looked fine until she turned the light on. "Oh."

Standing beside her, I took in what looked like someone had taken papier-mâché and made some kind of sculpture with it on the lower part of the wall. "What is that?"

She sighed. "The landlord agreed to let a new tenant move in as long as I left the place like I found it. Unfortunately, for a short period, I thought I would make a good dog sitter."

"And you ended up burying one of them in the wall?"

She playfully slapped my arm. "No. I left one of them loose and he ate the wall. I'm repairing it so I don't lose my deposit."

"I see."

"What do you see?"

"Your enthusiasm."

Hands to hips, she faced me.

I continued, "And dedication to the project. That's a lot of layers."

"Funny guy, huh?"

"And more than a little creativity."

With amused exasperation, she said, "Okay, so I'm not good at renovation. I almost hired someone, but . . ."

"But?"

She hesitated, then looked away. "I didn't want to be alone with anyone in my apartment."

A rush of protectiveness flooded in. I'd spoken enough to Shelby to understand how affected she'd been by the murder of her parents. It made sense that Megan would not feel safe with strangers in her home either. I fought back the urge to tell her she'd never have to face that alone because I'd be right there with her.

I held those words back because I wasn't in a position to make that kind of promise. I was a house guest in Boston and there was no way in hell I was going back to Driverton. "What else needs to be fixed?" I growled.

She misread my tone as irritation with her. "This isn't your problem. Worst case, I lose my deposit and maybe a month of rent."

"Show me what else needs fixing."

She searched my face. "Helping me pack is already more than enough."

"You won't lose a penny of your deposit. We'll take a drive to a hardware store, pick up some materials, then I'll make this place move-in ready. But I need to know what to buy."

Her mouth opened and shut a few times before she had me follow her back into the living room. "There's also a hole behind that painting. I tried to put up a security system and may have gotten a little aggressive with hammering when it kept falling off the wall."

I removed the painting and coughed on a laugh when I saw several nail holes that would have been easy enough to fill next to a larger hole that looked like she'd made it with the head of the hammer. "Do you have more of this paint?"

"I do. The landlord gave me some when I moved in."

"Then all of this will be easy. Let's go shopping."

"You sure?"

I ran my fingers gently through her hair. "There are a lot of things I don't yet know how to do, but I know how to do this. I can not only repair drywall and get your stuff into that storage container by tomorrow night, I can also make it fun."

"Really?" Desire darkened her eyes.

Tightening my hand into the hair at the nape of her neck, I murmured, "Young lady, is that where your mind always goes?"

"Around you? Yes." She didn't seem the least bit embarrassed.

We stood there, grinning at each other, and in that moment, it was impossible to imagine my life without her in it. We needed to be together. How it would happen or what it would look like—that was the only unclear part. "Go put your damn shoes on. This apartment won't pack itself."

"Yes, sir." Her laugh was beautifully lighthearted and mirrored how I felt. When she sashayed away it took all the strength in me to not go after her, swing her up into my arms, and put the packing off another day.

What held me back was an even stronger desire to care for her. Megan was both confident by nature and shaken to the core by circumstance. The men she'd chosen to fill her evenings with while she found her footing were damn lucky to have had her for as long as they did. I'll admit to some jealousy when she'd first told me about them, but the more I got to know her, the more I understood the stabilizing role they'd played in her journey. I couldn't resent them for giving her a sense of security when she'd needed it.

She was back moments later with her purse. "Ready?"

I was and I wasn't. When we'd met, I'd felt trapped by my life in Driverton. Boston had me feeling like a fledgling who'd wandered out onto a branch and was learning to flap its wings. To get where I wanted to go, I needed to leap and test myself.

How could I ask anyone to leap with me when I didn't know if I'd soar or crash and burn?

Chapter Twenty-Four

Megan

NOTE TO SELF, never move without an HHH: hot, hilarious, handyman.

Right out the gate, a generous amount of great sex is the perfect stress reducer. The piles of unassembled boxes had been a source of anxiety for me for the past week now represented a chance to spend more time with Ollie.

Ollie made good on his promise to make the process of moving fun. At the hardware store, when I'd walked over to the bubble wrap, his grin had been playful as he'd asked me if I was open to moving the way people in Driverton did.

Um, sure?

He bought supplies to patch the wall, tons of shrink wrap, paper plates, trash bags, and colorful duct tape. I tried to pay, but he wouldn't let me. Part of me wanted to protest that I had more disposable income than he did, but he was already carrying himself like someone who could afford to splurge, and I didn't want to take that away from him.

By the time we stopped at a large department store to pick up a zipline kit, I was fully invested. Each item he chose was accompanied by a story of who'd thought of it back in Driverton. I hadn't thought of the townspeople as being transient, but the younger population moved away for school and often moved back to raise a family. Packing and unpacking parties were something Ollie had participated in many times.

I noted, but didn't mention, that his face lit up whenever he talked about anyone from Driverton. His reasons for leaving were valid and I understood how he needed to follow the opportunities he was being offered. Still, though, it tugged at my heart that he felt he couldn't have both.

We were heading back to my apartment when he asked if there was a smoked barbeque place near me. I did a quick search on my phone and located one not too far away. I wasn't hungry yet, but I would be that evening.

When we walked into the restaurant, I imagined we'd order enough for the two of us. Instead, Ollie asked to speak to the owner. The man who came out from the back was a short and stocky, mostly bald man. The two of them shook hands and started talking like old friends. Ollie told him all about how I was moving and that he'd like to order enough of whatever was best on the menu so he could repay whichever neighbors decided to help us that day.

I touched Ollie's arm. "The people in my building aren't exactly . . . friendly."

He laid a hand over mine. "People can't help themselves. Something about a good barbeque brings out the friendly side of everyone."

I exchanged a look with the owner and sent him a silent plea. I didn't want Ollie to waste money on food no one in my building would eat. Hell, I'd lived there for years, and no one had ever so much as opened a door for me.

The owner snapped his fingers and said, "I have a food truck I use on the weekends. My son is home from school. I'll send him with some dishes. You pay for what we give out and it's a deal."

"My budget is five hundred dollars."

Five hundred dollars? My hand tightened on his arm. "Ollie, you don't have to do this."

He smiled down at me. "Pretend this is our first date and I'm taking you to an exclusive restaurant."

An older woman came out of the kitchen and in Spanish asked what was going on. My Spanish comprehension was beginner at best, but I understood that much. He answered too quickly for me to keep up. Whatever he said must have pleased her, though, because she beamed a huge smile at both of us. "You live around here?" she asked in English.

"I do." I wrinkled my nose. "But not for long. I'm moving to Maine."

"Ah, Maine. The land of the moose."

Ollie interjected, "I have a friend with a freezer full of moose meat. Would you like me to have some shipped down to you? It's lean and makes the best jerky."

The owner put an arm around the woman beside him. "Four hundred dollars, you send us some moose meat, and I'll cover anything we give out above $400." He and Ollie not only shook on it, but Ollie promised to spread the word about his place.

Two hours later, the lawn in front of my building looked like a street party. Music blared and people were scattered all around, many on blankets or towels they'd brought so they could eat picnic style. Above their heads, a zip line carried bags of items down to the POD where Ollie was standing.

He'd set up a process where people came to see me in my apartment first, received a box or something to carry down, brought it to him to receive a ticket that they then traded in at the food truck for a plate of food or a drink. The first one or two were skeptical, but as soon as people started saying how good the barbeque was, lines started to form. I couldn't pack fast enough to keep up, so people started to help me. The paper plates made packing my dishes easy enough. We color-coded the boxes for each room with different duct tape. My couches went down with some hungry young men who returned with friends for my tables and bedframe. The clothing I thought would take me forever to pack remained on hangers, went right into trash bags, then whoosh, slid down the zip line to Ollie.

When a police cruiser showed up, the music was turned off and the general mood of the crowd sank. Ollie left his spot and invited the officers over to the food truck. I watched from the window as he made introductions, then handed each officer a container of barbeque and a soda. They seemed to be asking questions, then one took a bite of a Brisket Grilled Cheese and made a face like the taste had sent him to heaven.

The music began again.

Standing with the police officers, Ollie pointed at me then waved. I waved back with a smile. The three of them stood there, looking comfortable in a way people in the city often didn't.

Even as I marveled at how skilled Ollie was with people, I realized it made sense that he would be. Little Willie's was where people went both for companionship and when in need. He'd spent his whole life nurturing a community. And it showed. People didn't just like him, they trusted him.

They weren't alone in that. Ollie had a good heart. What that meant as far as us, I didn't know, but I knew I wouldn't ever regret letting him into my life.

When everything but my luggage and Myrtle's habitat were packed into the storage container, I went down to the street. Everyone I spoke to was friendly and I wondered how different the building would have been if Ollie had lived there with me.

I was still recovering from that thought when Ollie took my hand and led me to the food truck so I could get a sample before it closed. The young man working the truck was a taller version of the restaurant owner. In no time Ollie had him talking about how he was going to school to be an engineer but had chosen to study close to his parents so he could continue to help out. They swapped stories about the pros and cons of essentially growing up in a restaurant.

I listened in fascination. There was a lot about Little Willie's that Ollie still loved, but since losing his father it wasn't the same for him. He didn't want to see it close, but he also dreaded his life revolving around keeping it open. The son of the smokehouse said that was something he emphatically understood.

When there was a lull in their conversation, I followed an impulse and asked, "Would you like help cleaning up?"

Ollie nodded in approval. "It's the least we could do."

At first the man looked about to refuse, then shrugged and motioned for us to join him in the food truck. Ollie encouraged me to share the reason I was moving, and soon, I was talking about my life's dreams while we all washed down the equipment.

The three of us laughed over how we were all trying to live up to our parents' expectations while at the same time failing. "I haven't told my parents yet that I quit my job or that I'm moving," I said.

"You should," Ollie said with a frown.

I shrugged. "I don't want to hear a lecture before I have time to decide for myself if it was the right move."

Ollie thanked our new friend and led me by the hand

out of the truck. We made our way through the thinning crowd of my neighbors up to my almost entirely empty apartment. Once inside, he wrapped his arms around me and gave me a long, heart-healing hug I'm pretty sure we both needed.

He raised his head. "You can't stay here tonight. Let's get the patching and the painting done and check into a hotel."

"I have a blow-up mattress, but I think we packed it. A hotel sounds heavenly."

"Will Myrtle be okay?"

"She eats every other day so she'll be fine if I give her something before we go."

He bent and growled into my ear. "Good, because unless you have other plans, you're mine until Monday morning."

Plans? No. Not a single one.

Chapter Twenty-Five

Ollie

MONDAY MORNING CAME too fast. I woke long before the sun came up because although I had a 9:00 a.m. meeting with Grant Barrington in Boston and a long drive back, I hadn't wanted to leave Megan a moment before I absolutely had to.

I was tempted to wake her, but she was sleeping peacefully so I wrote her a quick note and placed it beside her phone. After gathering my things, I ordered room service for her, coffee and blueberry pancakes because they were her favorite. While packing, I'd noticed she had a substantial collection of paperback books, so I'd slyly picked a new one up from the department store. As I checked out of the hotel, I arranged for that book and a bouquet of flowers to be delivered with her breakfast. I also hired a car to take her home when she woke. It was expensive, but to be the man I wanted to become, I needed to act the way he would.

There was no going back. A weekend with Megan had

shown me that. No excuses. No backsliding. The life I wanted to have was within my reach and so was Megan. One would require hard work, but I'd never been afraid of that. And Megan? I needed a plan.

I couldn't ask her to live with me while I was staying with Clay. I couldn't promise to take care of her when I wasn't yet in a better financial position. In the past, I'd often chosen quick fixes, but they hadn't gotten me far. The Barringtons had shown me that seeking comfort in immediate gratification was what had kept me in a cycle of failure and frustration.

So, sure, staying with Megan instead of returning to Boston would have felt good, but that wouldn't have been a solid foundation for us to build a relationship on. Returning to Driverton to be closer to her and those I cared about also wouldn't have put me in a position where I could support my mother, keep Little Willie's open, and buy a home for the family Megan would likely want to have.

I have a plan, Megan.

All I need is a little time to make it happen.

My weekend with Megan had shown me how good life would be with her at my side. In and out of bed, we fit in a way I'd never thought possible. She could read my mind at times. We belonged together. Scary, but incredible as well.

I was returning to Boston no longer asking myself if I could do this, but how I would.

That's why the note I wrote her said: **Thank you.**

Chapter Twenty-Six

>>>«««

Megan

Waking up alone should have been something I felt comfortable with. I'd lived on my own ever since I'd left home at eighteen. This past year, I'd spent a night or two with a man, but it hadn't been at my place. I'm sure a therapist could unravel why, although I didn't want to be alone, I hadn't felt comfortable allowing a man into my space while I slept.

Until Ollie.

Moving closer to Driverton was about healing the side of me that didn't feel safe alone. Was being with Ollie a step forward or a step back? I couldn't tell.

The note he'd left by my phone did nothing to alleviate my confusion. I called Shelby as soon as I found it. "Thank you? *Thank you?* What kind of man leaves a Thanks-for-a-good-fuck note and sneaks out?" I didn't need to tell her who I was referring to. We texted each other daily and Ollie's visit was the only reason she and Everette hadn't been there to help. We'd decided that although more hands were better when it came to moving, Ollie and I would benefit more from some one-on-one time.

She gasped. "Ollie wrote that?"

I groaned. "Not in those exact words, but he did leave before I woke."

"Read me the note."

I flapped it in front of me and read it dramatically. "Thank you. Ollie" I turned the note over before waving it through the air again. "That's it. What the hell is he thanking me for? The sex? Or is this a Thank-you-we're-done note? And then to leave while I'm still sleeping? I wouldn't even treat a fuck buddy like that."

"You have fuck buddies?"

"Not lately," I said impatiently. "Focus. I just had an incredible weekend with Ollie. If you'd asked me last night if we had a future together, I would have said absolutely. I've never been with someone I feel so connected to. Sometimes I feel like I can read his mind and see right into his heart. And then he does this bullshit and I think . . . do I know him at all?"

"I'm going to need a coffee and more information. You told me you had a good weekend, but walk me through it."

I did. I took her all the way back to us getting hot and heavy as soon as he appeared at my door, to why I was in a hotel room a few miles from my apartment.

"That all sounds amazing."

"I know. Being with him feels *right*."

"But?"

"Thank you?"

"You could text him and ask him what he was thinking."

"What are my other options?"

She chuckled. "Well . . . I could ask Everette what he thinks Ollie meant by that."

"Hang on. Someone's knocking." I went near the hotel room door. "Who is it?"

"Room service."

I whispered to Shelby. "I didn't order any. Should I open the door?"

"Tell them that."

"Good idea." Through the closed door, I said, "I'm sorry, I didn't order room service."

"Mr. Williams did for you. He also left instructions for what was to be delivered with it."

"FaceTime me," Shelby said urgently. "I need to see this."

I switched to video and opened the door. The woman pushed a cart through the doorway and over to the end of the bed. With some quick adjustments the rectangular rolling cart became a round table that she placed a white tablecloth over. From beneath the cart, she pulled out a vase of forget-me-nots, a carafe of coffee, a glass of orange juice, and a stack of blueberry pancakes. I was already getting teary when the woman handed me a gift-wrapped paperback book. I gave the woman a hefty tip and she asked if there was anything else I needed before leaving me standing there in wonder.

"He got me a book." I sniffed and propped my phone against a lamp so Shelby could watch as I removed the wrapping. "It's a romance." After reading the back, I said, "A friends-to-lovers and it's by Melody Anne—one of my favorite authors. I'm so excited. I've been wanting to get this one. I think I told him about her a while back."

"Sounds like Ollie notices what you like."

I hugged the book to my chest as my attention returned to what had been delivered. "I'm seeing a pattern. This is the second time he's given me forget-me-nots. Is that a hint?"

"A romantic one."

I stepped closer to the cart and smiled. "Blueberry pancakes. I told him I love them."

"You can probably forgive him now for the brevity of the note. The book and the flowers required planning. Some men go on and on about how much they care, but their actions don't reflect that. Ollie is showing you he cares. If it takes time for his words to catch up . . . I think that's okay."

"He did tell me he had to be back in Boston for an early meeting." Still hugging the book, I sat on the edge of the bed and looked into the eyes of my best friend. "He looks good, Shelby. And when I say that I don't mean more muscled and polished. He's standing taller, looking more self-assured and comfortable with himself. If he offered to give all that up for me, I wouldn't want him to, but I want him to want to . . .

for me. Does that make any sense?"

"Yes and no."

"He didn't ask me for anything this time, but I know he still needs time. God, I wish that was an easier thing to give him." I breathed in deeply. "I miss him, Shelby. I don't think about any of the men I've left behind, but I miss Ollie so much I ache. And I don't know what to do with that."

"You could go to him."

"And do what? Get a job in Boston? Ask him to take one closer to me? I don't want to give up on the turtle sanctuary before I've experienced what working at one is like. And I don't want to be what stops Ollie from reaching for his own dreams."

"Your mother once said something to me that I wrote off as her not knowing what she was talking about. It was at your high school graduation party. I was upset that some guy I had a crush on hadn't shown up."

"Noah?"

"Yes. Him. Anyway, I was sulking. She told me to quit blaming someone else for what was my own responsibility. Happiness isn't something someone can give or take away. We choose how we feel. I wrote that off as annoying advice when I least wanted to hear some, but I think she was right. I'm much happier since Everette has come into my life, not because he makes me happy, but because he encouraged me to discover what I needed to be happy again."

"Ollie loves the idea of me working at the sanctuary."

"Because he knows what it'll mean to you. Just like you know what being in Boston means to him."

"Yeah."

"I'm sorry, Megan. I know this is hard."

"It is, but it's also . . . beautiful." I sat down beside the cart. "Do you think we'll end up together?"

"I don't know, Megan, but I'd like to think so."

"Me too."

Me too.

A moment later, I blurted, "Hey, one more thing."

"Yes?"

"When we hang up, I'm going to call my parents and tell them I'm moving."

"Good."

"Whatever they think about it will be okay, because I need to do this for me."

"Exactly."

"And I miss them."

"Of course you do."

"They wanted me to move back home after what happened to your parents. We both said some hurtful things."

"I remember."

"I didn't mean any of it. I was angry and not with them—with myself for wanting to go home and hide. I didn't want to be that person."

"I'm sure they didn't mean what they said either. Although I miss my parents every day, we didn't always get along—you know that. Relationships are complicated, but if

I had a chance to go back and apologize to my parents for the silly things I said when I was angry with them I would. Losing them was what made me realize how little most of what we worried about mattered."

"You've got your shit together more than I do right now. Maybe *you* should call my mother," I joked.

Shelby laughed. "You've got this. Hey. I have to go. Call me later."

I WAS IN my new apartment, setting up Myrtle's habitat, when Shelby called. "Still waiting for my stuff," I answered cheerfully. "The shipping storage container is en route but stuck in traffic."

"Megan," the urgency in her voice had me instantly on alert. "Levi just received bad news regarding his parents."

"His parents? I thought he wasn't in contact with them."

"He hasn't heard from them in about a decade, but Clay located them. Or Bradford did. I'm not sure. Anyway, from what I understand they were living on an island off the coast of Florida and recently drowned."

My legs started shaking so badly I sank to the carpeted floor and just sat there. "Was it . . . were they . . . was it an accident?"

"From what Bradford told us, yes. They worked for a resort and were ferrying guests to the island. Levi's mother fell overboard and his father dove in to save her. Neither one survived. There were witnesses."

Hand to mouth, I blinked back tears. "That's horrific. How did Levi take the news?"

"About as good as could be expected. Katie is making him dinner. Everette is going to give them some time together before he tells Ollie."

"Why wouldn't he tell him right away?"

"You know how Ollie feels about Levi showing any interest in his cousin. With them getting closer while Ollie has been away and now this... it's a powder keg waiting to explode."

I did know how protective Ollie was of his younger cousin. After my call with Shelby ended, I was conflicted. On one hand, it didn't feel right to keep the news from Ollie. On the other hand, I also didn't want to set him up for a blowout with his best friend. Especially when Ollie's other closest friend thought it was best to give Levi time to process the loss first with Katie.

Levi's parents are dead.

Shelby's as well.

And here I am avoiding calling mine because I'm afraid they'll say the wrong thing?

When do we get past that stage?

Are they not calling me for the same reason?

I thought about what Cole said; we had been holding each other back. Was I doing the same with my parents? But, instead of breaking it off with them, did I have to reassess what I was bringing to them?

They knew nothing about my move or what had led me

to decide to. Without that information, the move might appear impulsive and irrational.

Taking a deep breath, I called my mother. She answered on the first ring. "Megan, is everything okay?"

"Yes. I'm fine. I'm just calling to say hello."

"Oh, good. Your father and I were talking about you yesterday. We're thinking about popping over for a visit soon. There's that quaint bed and breakfast place not too far from you and it has vacancies next weekend and the following one. How do you feel about having some company?"

"Before you book a room, there's something I need to tell you . . . actually, there's a lot I should have told you sooner . . ."

A short time later, I was feeling emotionally wiped, but in a good way. News of the death of Levi's parents had changed the way I'd both shared my news and received my parents' concerned questions. I took the plunge and told my mother the last year had been rough on me. From what had happened to Shelby's parents, to worrying about Shelby as she'd teetered, to realizing I wasn't happy with the life I'd made for myself. Moving to Maine represented the fresh start I needed.

My mother's questions reflected not only her concerns about the new neighborhood I was moving into but also that I hadn't given them any indication I was struggling. There was a time, not long ago, when I would have gotten defensive and interpreted each of her questions as a lack of trust in me.

I remembered the conversation Ollie and I had had with the son of the food truck owner. All three of us felt that we were disappointing our parents.

But were we?

Maybe they only want the best for us and worry.

Maybe all we need to do is not guess the motivation behind a question and just answer it.

Near the end of our conversation, my mother asked if I was seeing anyone.

I chose to not read anything into that question. Instead, I was honest. "Yes and no."

She made a tsk sound. "You either are or you aren't."

"It's complicated."

"Not when it's right, it's not. Is he married?"

"Mom! Of course not."

"Dating someone else?"

"Not that I'm aware of. No."

"Then what's the issue?"

"He's . . . I'm . . . we're both trying to get ourselves in a better place mentally and financially before we get serious."

"Oh."

I couldn't tell from that if she approved or not. "He has some business opportunities that are drawing him to Boston. Meanwhile, I'm more and more drawn to Driverton and a new career."

"Driverton. Where Shelby is?"

"Yes."

"What are you not telling me?"

"I can't imagine. I feel like you know everything now."

"Where is this man you're waiting to be serious about from?"

"Driverton."

"Is that where you see him?"

"Not anymore, but I do stay with his mother when I visit Shelby."

"His *mother*?" Her voice rose an octave.

"Yes, she runs a sort of unofficial bed and breakfast. She's also a wonderful human being. You'd like her."

"And what does she think of you and her son?"

"She says she wants both of us to be happy whether we end up together or not."

"I like that. Do you think she'd have a room open this coming weekend?"

I inhaled sharply. "This weekend? I don't know. That's short notice." And potentially bad timing as far as meeting everyone. There was no way to explain that, though, without going into detail about things that were not my place to discuss.

"If you'd rather your father and I don't come, you can say it, but we'd like to see you and this place you're drawn to."

What I'd say next felt like it would pivot my relationship one way or the other. I could let them in and hope they supported the new life I was designing for myself, or I could protect it from them and reduce seeing them to a few times a year. "It's a crazy town, full of crazy people . . . but I kind of love it. The only thing stopping me from moving there is the lack of employment opportunity."

"Which is why . . . what's your man's name?"

"Ollie."

"Which is why Ollie is in Boston."

"Yes. For now. The original plan was for him to learn a skill he could return home and make a career from, but more opportunities seem to be opening to him."

"Sounds like you found yourself a motivated man. How would you feel about moving to Boston if he asked you?"

I sighed. "We're not at that point, Mom."

When she didn't respond to that, I made a decision. "Mrs. Williams loves company. I'll check with her, but I bet she'd enjoy you visiting this coming weekend. And so would I."

Long after ending the call with my mother, I restlessly paced my new place. Instead of an apartment building, I'd moved into a duplex in a family-friendly neighborhood. Everything about the area was wholesome and inviting, but I wasn't yet sure how I felt about being there.

Life is a combination of wonderful and horrible happenings crammed in a blender and spun into a confusing soup of . . . just a lot. Too much to know what to do with sometimes.

A knock interrupted my thoughts. *My stuff must be here!* When I opened my door, I was greeted by a driver who wanted to know where he could drop the container. I pointed to the grassy area beside the driveway. As he walked away a group of four women came up my steps. They all wore matching blue T-shirts that read: Mindy's Movers and Cleaning Services. One of them held a paper out to me. It was an invoice for them to unload and organize my things paid for by Oliver Williams.

Presumptuous.

Over the top.

But such a welcome gift.

With a huge smile on my face, I ushered the women inside and showed them where I'd like the furniture and boxes to go. After the tour, they said they prep a house before bringing things in and headed out to their vehicle to gather their cleaning supplies.

I took advantage of being left on my own to send Ollie a text: **Thank you.**

I did smirk as I hit send.

His response came back quickly. **Next best thing to being there to help you myself.**

You're going to spoil me.

Do you have a problem with that?

Not at all.

The driver interrupted to ask for a signature. By the time he left, my house was chaotic with the cleaning crew. I felt guilty doing nothing while they worked, but I didn't know which box contained my cleaning supplies, so I stepped outside, telling myself I'd help carry things in. **Guess what? I talked to my mom today and she and my father want to visit**

Driverton.
That's fantastic. Have them stay with my mom. She'll love meeting them.

Had he really just accepted the idea of our parents meeting as if it was nothing? Did that mean he saw us as being at that stage? Or the opposite? Was being serious with me so far off his radar that he didn't see how them meeting might be a big step? I wanted to ask him, but there was something more pressing I could no longer hold back. Right or wrong, I couldn't keep a secret from him.

You need to call Everette. He has news about Levi.
I know. He called me.
Oh, good.
I'm heading home tomorrow morning. Everette is with him tonight and I want to meet with the Barringtons before I leave. They've moved their schedules around to accommodate me, the least I can do is explain in person why I'm leaving.
They'll understand.
Even if they don't, Levi means more to me than anything here ever could.

And that, folks, is the moment I knew I loved Ollie.
How long do you think you'll stay?
As long as I need to.

I took a deep breath before typing: **You'll probably see me there.**
I'd love that.
He'd love that.
Should I stay at a hotel?
And offend my mother? No.

It wasn't his mother's feelings I'd been thinking about. Although, I was tempted to ask what he'd told his mother about us. But what if he said nothing? I wished I could reach through the phone and shake him until he told me what I meant to him.

Instead, I wrote: **Since unpacking won't be the huge feat I thought it would be, I might head to Driverton Wednesday. I don't start my job until next week.**

See you then.

Gripping my phone, I let out a little frustrated scream. One of the moving women asked me if I was okay. I shot her an apologetic smile and said, "Just trying to figure my man out."

She waved a hand in understanding. "Let it out, honey. We're all right there with you. I've been married for eight years, and I've made that very sound into a pillow more than once. I love my husband, but if he puts his dirty socks on the counter near my toothbrush one more time, I may strangle him with them."

I gurgled on a laugh I released only when she started laughing. After choosing a box to carry back to the house, I asked, "Do you have any regrets?"

She picked up a box as well. "About getting married? No. We drive each other crazy sometimes, but he's my best friend."

We walked into the house together. "How did you know he was the one?"

She smiled and for a moment looked lost in memories.

"We were dating. He started working the night shift which meant we didn't see as much of each other, but every time it snowed he drove over after work to shovel my driveway and clean off my car. That did something to my heart, you know? It didn't cost him anything and maybe wouldn't impress other women, but it made me feel . . . treasured. A decade later, he still goes out of his way to show me how much I mean to him."

"That's beautiful. You should keep him."

"Oh, I intend to." She placed the box down inside the house and turned toward me. "I don't know what your man did, but the fact that he hired us to help you unpack should tell you all you need to know."

My heart skipped at the idea that Ollie could be saying with actions what he couldn't with words. *I believe in you, Ollie, and I want to believe in us.*

Chapter Twenty-Seven

Ollie

DAYS LATER, I parked my car near my father's gravesite but didn't immediately move to get out. I'd been home for two days and although it was nice to see everyone, I was ready to leave. Outside of the fact that Levi and I had nearly ended a lifelong friendship when I'd found out he and Katie were now a couple, everything was just as I'd left it.

Nothing had changed.

Except me.

Katie was right, though, about why I'd dreaded the idea of my best friend and my cousin getting together. Nothing bad usually happened in Driverton, but we'd almost lost Katie a few years earlier to a creep who'd lured her away then turned violent.

The day Cooper and Pete had brought her home, bloody and bruised from that monster's hands, was one I'd never fully gotten over. We all wanted to kill him. Tom had convinced us that the beating Cooper had given him was already going to be difficult to cover up. A murder would have put what happened to Katie in the news—and her welfare was all that mattered.

So, yeah, I may have become protective of my little cousin. And Levi? As much as I loved him, when his parents had up and left town without him, it had done something to him. He had a reputation for not staying with any woman long.

He was broken and we both knew it. That was why I'd asked him to swear to me he'd never touch Katie. Apparently that promise had proven impossible to keep.

Katie wasn't a child, and I believed him when he said he'd never hurt her. There really was no other choice than to accept their decision and hope he'd keep the promises he was making to her better than he'd kept the one he'd made me.

He did look like he was in love with her, and I knew how confusing that could be. If I wasn't waiting for Megan to arrive that evening, I would have already left Driverton. Everette and Cooper said they'd watch Little Willie's. I'd visited with my mother, seen my friends, and spoken to half the town.

There was nothing left for me there. At least, that's how it felt.

I let myself out of my truck and sank to my knees in front of my father's headstone. "I wish you were here. You'd like Megan. Mom enjoys being with her almost more than I do." I breathed in deeply. "I've been sober now for over a month. Things are going well." My hand fisted against the stone. "So why is being here torture? I don't get it. Why does coming home hurt like this?"

My hand fell from the headstone when he didn't answer. Had I expected him to? No. No rational part of me had anyway. Maybe one small fucking corner of my soul had held out the hope that he could.

"I thought I might find you here," Pete said from a short distance away.

I didn't rise to greet him. "I'm fine, Pete. Just sorting through some shit."

He dropped to a seated position beside me. "Is this about Katie and Levi getting together?"

"No. We talked that through and I'm over it. I don't want to see her get hurt, but they really care about each other. I won't stand in the way of that."

"Good call." He cleared his throat. "I hear you've been doing really well in Boston. Everyone's proud of you."

I shot him a side glance. "You know why I had to go."

"I do. Everyone does, but that doesn't make us less proud. Clay told me you're a natural businessman. He thinks you'll do well in whatever you choose to do next."

"He's gone above and beyond to help me."

"Bradford speaks highly of you as well."

"I don't give a fuck about Bradford."

Pete coughed. "How are you handling being home?"

I shrugged. "It's fine. It's good to see everyone."

"Don't lie to me, son. I know you too well for that."

That was damn sure. I turned and shifted so I was seated as well. "Being home doesn't feel good anymore."

He nodded "The tough thing about a small town is that your mistakes linger on display like a mural you can't paint over. I've stumbled more than a few times in my life and when I did it was damn tempting to go somewhere where no one would have an opinion about it. Thankfully Dotty kept my ass here."

"Everything I want is out there... not here." Unless Megan chose to move to Driverton. No, I didn't want to think about that possibility.

He sighed. "You can live wherever you want to, but one place doesn't need to nullify another. Sure, if you're seeking money and power, you won't find it here. But are you sure that's what will make you happy?"

"It's better than working seven days a week and never getting ahead."

"And what will you do with the money you make?"

"I'll keep my promises to my father. His goal was to take care of his family and the people in Driverton. Levi is heading down to Florida today to find out if his parents left him their house. If they didn't, he'll need to find a place to live. Flat broke, I can't help him. I hate that. That's not how I want to live and now I know I don't have to. At least, when I'm in Boston I know that. Everything is different there. *I'm different.*"

"Not too different, I hope." After a moment, he added, "Even if Levi's parents didn't leave him the house, he'll be okay. We'll make sure of that. The weight of the world doesn't rest solely on your shoulders."

I nodded, even though sometimes that wasn't how it felt.

He said, "No matter where your journey takes you, remember we're your family, your home, and your strength. You're never alone."

That was how I wanted to feel about Driverton again. I looked at my father's headstone then back at Pete. "How do you always know when I need to talk?"

"Your father asked me to look after you. He nudges me in your direction now and then. You have anything you want to tell him? I feel him here with us."

Whether that was true or not, I wanted it to be. "Dad, I'm trying to do better. Help me get this right."

Pete put a hand on my shoulder. "You will." He used my shoulder to leverage himself back to standing.

I rose to my feet as well. "Thanks, Pete. For everything."

He smiled. "Like I said, we're each other's strength. I wouldn't still be here without your father and the talks he gave me when I struggled. I'm not proud of the dark places my memories sometimes take me, but he taught me to be kinder to myself when they do."

"He was a good man."

"The best." Pete clapped a hand on my back. "And so are you. Don't let anything you find out there make you forget that."

Chapter Twenty-Eight

⋙⋘

Megan

It was disappointing to not be met by Ollie when I arrived at his house, but the long hug his mother gave me on the porch helped me put that aside. When she released me, she was grinning from ear to ear. "Clay called and asked everyone to meet at Little Willie's. He has an announcement to make."

"What do you think it's about?"

"I have no idea, but he sounded happy. Really happy. People are already gathering. No time to settle in." She opened the door and pointed to the side. "Put your bag down and let's go."

"Well, okay, then." I placed my bag inside. She closed the door as soon as my arm was clear of it.

After handing me the keys to her car, she climbed into the passenger seat of her vehicle. I would have offered to drive her in mine, but she was too fast for me.

On the way she updated me on how Bradford had flown

Levi and Katie down to Florida to meet with a lawyer. "I heard it was on a private plane. Enormous and fancy." She lowered her voice to a confidential tone. "Levi told me Bradford borrowed it from Dominic Corisi. Do you know who he is?"

"Doesn't everyone?"

"And now Levi is staying at his house with him."

"With Dominic Corisi?"

"Yes." Her voice went even lower. "I've been reading about him. There's a lot of conspiracy theories about how he made his money. They say no one speaks ill of him because no one who has lived to do it twice."

Whispering as well for no reason other than I was finding this amusing, I asked, "Why do you sound so excited about that? Shouldn't we be scared for Levi?"

"Everette told me Levi told him Bradford only involved this Corisi man because he wanted to outdo Clay." She rolled her eyes. "Those two are like toddlers in a sandbox trying to outdo each other by having the biggest dump truck. I had no idea Bradford had any pettiness in him, but I have to say I like him more because of it."

"Why more?"

"Because I don't trust a man who acts like he has everything figured out. Bradford's been spouting wisdom and putting people through his training program like he's building a cult following. This ridiculous show of male pride is proof he's human and no better than the rest of us."

"I get that. I guess. But I don't understand how that's exciting."

She smiled and sat straighter. "Then you don't know Clay as well as I do. He won't let Bradford outdo him. I don't know what he's planning, but it'll be a show we won't want to miss."

My parents can wait another week before they come here. Yeah. That's probably for the best.

The parking lot of Little Willie's was indeed packed when we arrived. Every table was occupied and the spaces around them filled with more people standing. A good portion of them greeted me as we walked in, and I hugged several of them.

Shelby was standing with Everette near the bar. She waved me over to join her. Reana took a seat a young man offered her.

"What is this about?" I asked as soon as I was in earshot of Everette and Shelby.

"With Clay who knows," Everette said with a smile.

Shelby pulled me in for a hug. "I tried to get Lexi to give me a clue, but she's tight-lipped."

As soon as she released me, I scanned the room.

Everette's expression turned sympathetic. "Ollie's been MIA most of the day."

I didn't bother to pretend he wasn't correct in his assumption that I was looking for him. "I'm sure he'll show up."

"He will. You're the only reason he's still here." Everette

sighed. "The rest of us just annoy him lately."

"I'm sure you don't." I accepted the soda Shelby handed me. "He's annoyed with himself, not you."

With the saddest expression I'd ever seen on a grown man, Everette said, "I bet the next time he leaves, he's not coming back."

I shook my head in denial but froze when I met Shelby's gaze. Her tone was gentle. "He doesn't want to be here anymore."

I scanned the room again. Ollie loved these people. He lit up every time he talked about them. Why wouldn't he love being with them? And then it hit me. "He's scared."

"What?" Everette asked.

I continued, "He's afraid to fail. He's done that here . . . again and again . . . at least in his mind he has. But he hasn't in Boston. I bet a part of him thinks the longer he's here the more likely he won't succeed out there."

Everette frowned. "That doesn't make sense."

Shelby slipped beneath one of his arms and hugged him. "It doesn't have to. Fear never does. I understand that well."

He kissed the top of her head. "Then we'll have to find a way to help him conquer that fear, because I'm not giving him up without a fight."

Eyes blurring with tears, I nodded in approval. "He's lucky to have you in his life."

Everette shrugged. "I feel the same about having him in mine. He's my brother from another mother. We've been through a lot together."

"And he's here," Shelby said.

My breath caught in my throat as I turned in the direction she was looking. Across the room, he nodded to me and cut through the crowd of people without ever breaking eye contact. I clasped my hands in front of me as my heart thudded wildly in my chest.

He didn't slow until he was right in front of me then cupped my face between his hands and gave me the kind of welcoming kiss I'd waited my whole life for. Had we been alone, it would have gone on forever. Instead, it ended too soon. I let out a sad sigh when he raised his head.

"It's good to see you," he said huskily.

I blinked back tears and smiled up at him. "It's good to see you too."

A little old lady across the room called out, "You'd better have locks on the doors at your place, Reana, or your house will be rocking back and forth tonight."

"My son knows better than that," Reana said staunchly.

"I do," Ollie said, smiling down at me. "Even this was too much."

I shook my head. "No, it was perfect."

He lowered his hands then laced one of them with mine. "Weren't you supposed to get here later tonight?"

I looked down then met his gaze again. "I couldn't wait any longer."

He hugged me to his chest and buried his face in my

hair. "Good, because I was having the same issue."

Heaven. His embrace was heaven. Nothing else came close to mattering when I was in his arms.

The sound of silverware being tapped against a glass quieted the room and people turned to where Clay was standing with his wife. "If I could have everyone's attention."

Reluctantly I shifted so I could see him better. Katie's parents were standing to one side of him. Bradford and Joanna were on his other.

Clay's voice carried throughout the room. "We've received exciting news from Levi and Katie. First, his parents did leave him the house."

Applause and cheering echoed through the room. I hugged Ollie so tight I'm surprised he didn't complain.

Clay continued, "But, more importantly, we've all been invited to stay at the home of Dominic Corisi and bear witness to Levi proposing tomorrow."

Katie's parents looked adorably excited, which made me happy for Levi. I knew he was concerned they might have reservations about him, but that wasn't what their expressions were saying.

I might have missed the little smirk Clay shot Bradford had Reana not brought their little competition with each other to my attention. Bradford's eyes narrowed as if daring Clay to proceed. Clay didn't seem the least bit deterred by the look. His voice was cheerful as he glanced down at his wife then around at the crowd again. "So, it is my pleasure to offer everyone here a flight to Florida and back so none of us miss this monumental moment."

Lexi smiled at Clay. "I love engagement parties and, if the Corisis are hosting, I bet the guest list will be impressive."

Shelby said, "I can look into getting us a group discount."

Clay tipped his head to one side as if she'd spoken in a language he didn't know, and I slapped her playfully on the hip. "I don't think Clay is flying us down on a commercial airline."

Clay frowned. "Oh. Is that how you'd prefer to fly? I can arrange that if you want, but I had something nicer in mind. There are quite a few of you. It would require several private planes or I could rent out a commercial plane I suppose. But aren't the seats on those crammed together?"

Bradford covered his face with one hand, shaking his head back and forth. Joanna elbowed him and reminded him to be nice.

I looked up at Ollie and in a voice intended for all to hear asked, "Ollie, what do you think? You have one foot in both worlds. What should we do?"

He cleared his throat and looked around. As he did, his shoulders squared. "There are pros and cons to both. However, if Clay is okay with the added expense of hiring more than one aircraft, I believe private would provide more comfort, especially for our less mobile." A grin spread across his face. "Plus, it's pretty fucking amazing."

"Language," his mother chided.

"I vote for fucking amazing," the little old woman who'd teased Reana earlier called out.

"Me too," the tiny bald man beside her said.

A murmur of agreement grew into a thundering expression of gratitude and excitement. Ollie said, "Looks like all of Driverton now has its own Fairy Godfather."

"*Extraordinaire.*" Lexi supplied the last part of Clay's title.

Clay's chest puffed with pride.

Bradford grumbled.

I hugged Ollie tightly again and smiled up at him. "Is this really happening?"

He hugged me back and said, "Bet your cute little ass it is."

Clay's voice rang out above the hum of the crowd again. "The Corisis host fancy parties. If you allow me, when we get down there, I'll add a little magic to the experience and in no time have you all looking like you often party with royalty and dignitaries."

"Could I have my nails done?" one woman asked.

"Absolutely," Clay answered.

A middle-aged woman next to Reana asked, "I wore my hair in an updo for my wedding. Could we have our hair done as well?"

Clay brought a hand to his chest and looked like he was

fighting back tears. "It would be my honor to make sure each of you has whatever would make this trip magical for you."

"Will the prince you flew in for Megan be there? If so, could my daughter who's in college come too?"

"It's not my party, but I can inquire if he's already on the list."

"He'd better not be," Ollie grumbled, and my gaze flew to meet his.

Jealous? I never thought I could find that hot, but I liked that Ollie saw me as his.

Shelby interjected, "I wonder if he's still heartbroken."

Ollie's eyebrows arched.

I raised and lowered a shoulder then fluttered my eyelashes at him. "Don't give me that look; I sent all his gifts back."

"Gifts? What did he send you?" Ollie didn't even attempt to hide his displeasure.

I told myself I shouldn't say it. My goal up until then was to make him feel better about himself, but the fire in his eyes was turning me on and I couldn't help myself. "Just jewelry and a car. Nothing big. He seemed to think I'd make a good princess . . ."

"Did he?" His nostrils flared.

"And I was tempted, but—"

In my ear, he growled. "Want to get out of here?"

Desire slashed through me even as I said, "We can't leave in the middle of Clay's speech."

"We can," he said. "There's a hotel not too far away. Say yes and I'll spend the whole night fucking the memory of that prince right out of you."

"Yes," I whispered, because no wasn't a word that was possible when every inch of me was craving every inch of him.

Chapter Twenty-Nine

Ollie

*L*IFE DOESN'T GET *stranger than this.* Dressed in a dark suit with a gorgeously done-up Megan at my side, I scanned the marbled ballroom and marveled at how different everyone appeared. Clay had promised he could make all of us look like we belonged there, and he'd pulled it off. If Mike and Mel hadn't walked around with a mason jar of moonshine, I would have thought they'd attended fancy parties regularly.

Levi had just proposed to Katie, and we were all basking in the aftermath of the beauty of that moment. Still, when I proposed to Megan, and I intended to, I didn't want it to be this formal. I pictured the two of us laughing and teasing each other while my mother looked on and scolded us for not being more serious.

I bent and kissed Megan's temple. She and I had things we needed to work out, but I was confident we could. She needed to come with me to Boston.

Images of how we'd fallen asleep all tangled around each other and woken the same way brought a smile to my face and bolstered my confidence that I could get her to agree to move to the city with me.

Not right away. First, I had to get my own place, and to do that, I needed to apply some of what I'd learned to something that would actually bring in money.

Megan caught me looking at her. "What are you thinking about?"

"You," I answered without hesitation. "All the damn time."

She wrinkled her nose. "I may be suffering from a similar affliction. Do you think anyone would mind if we slipped away later?"

"I don't care who minds, do you?"

"Not one damn bit."

We shared a smile like two kids conspiring to sneak out after curfew.

"Excuse me," a deep voice said, and I reluctantly looked away from Megan.

"Mr. Corisi," I said in surprise.

"Dominic, please. You're staying in my home." He smiled at Megan. "And who do I have the pleasure of meeting?"

Megan held out her hand to him. "Megan Gassett."

He shook her hand, then said, "Megan, would you mind if I borrowed your friend for a moment? I've heard good things about him and have a proposition if he's looking for work."

My jaw dropped. "For me?"

Dominic's smile was as smooth as one would expect from someone who'd likely lost count of how many zeros there were in his net worth. "I suppose I can spill the beans here. Every once in a while I come across someone with such integrity and character that I feel compelled to mentor them. Clay speaks highly of you, and I understand he's been helping you network, but nothing he's offered you so far has been concrete. I'd like to see what you'd do with a million dollars."

"A million?" My voice cracked.

"You're right. That's not enough to start up anything of importance. A hundred million. That's how much I'm willing to invest in you if you allow me to mentor you for six months. At the end of that time, either you'll have doubled that amount and I'll consider your debt to me paid or you'll have lost it, and our association will dissolve."

It sounded too good to be true. I met Megan's gaze. She smiled and shook my arm. "This is your chance. You can do this."

I inhaled deeply then looked Dominic in the eye. "I'm willing to look over whatever offer you're willing to put in writing."

He barked out a laugh. "Of course. I'll have papers to you in the morning."

I held out a hand to him, damned if mine didn't shake a little in his. *Fuck.* This was an unbelievable opportunity. Did I know what I was doing? Hell no. But I wasn't going to allow myself to fail because I was too afraid to try. "Thank you."

As soon as he was out of sight, I took both of Megan's hands in mine and we did a giddy little dance. "Is this real?" I asked.

She was all smiles. "I think so."

I hugged her to me. "If so, it'll make everything we want possible. Not immediately. I've heard his headquarters are in New York City. I'll probably have to head down there for a while."

Megan tensed against me.

I quickly added, "You'd come with me, of course."

She opened her mouth to say something then seemed to decide against it. "It's an amazing opportunity for you."

"For *us*," I said.

She nodded but didn't look me in the eye. I understood. All of it was still a shock to me as well. If she wasn't ready, I'd take things with her at whatever speed she needed me to. What mattered the most, though, was I'd just been given a real shot at success.

A few minutes later, Megan slipped away to the ladies' room and Bradford approached me. He didn't look happy, but that wasn't anything new. "What did Dominic Corisi say to you?"

"He offered to mentor me."

"Shit," Bradford said. "I realize that the temptation to say yes to him will be strong, but—"

"You don't think I'm good enough to work with him?"

"I didn't say that."

"But you think it."

"Listen, you have to know that people like him don't just offer to mentor people—"

"Like me. Say it. I know what you think of me. I wasn't good enough to work with you so why would someone like Dominic show any interest in me? I don't know what his motivation is, but if he's willing to give me a chance, I'm damn well going to take it. This would not only change my life, but the lives of everyone I care about. So, if you've got nothing positive to say, do me a favor and fuck off, Bradford."

He raised a hand in my direction then stormed off. Good. I didn't need him.

Things were turning around for me.

Six months and I'd be able to not only buy a beautiful home for Megan, but I could set up perpetual scholarships for anyone in Driverton who wanted to attend college. I could meet the Barringtons for a meal and be able to pay the tab for once. Little Willie's wouldn't close. My mother would never know that our family had ever had money issues.

This is happening.
It's really happening.

Chapter Thirty

Megan

Present Day

LITTLE WILLIE'S HAD undergone some upgrades since Levi and Katie had purchased it from Ollie. The booths were new. Wobbly chairs had been replaced. The tablecloths were bright and cheerful. Overall, it had been freshened up. Gone was the slight musty bar smell. What hadn't changed was that it remained where people in Driverton gathered, me included.

"You look exhausted," Reana said from across the table.

"Thanks?" I joked weakly. I was not only tired, but jetlagged as well. Going back to my house would have made more sense, especially since I had an early shift at the turtle sanctuary. However, since rehoming Myrtle to the sanctuary's extensive indoor habitat, my side of the duplex felt empty. She was thriving there, though, and that's what mattered.

"How are your parents?" she asked.

"Looking forward to coming for another visit next week. Are you up to having company again?"

"Are *you*?"

"Yes, actually. It's good to have them back in my life. And better now that they're no longer laying down rules and worrying about me."

"Parents never stop worrying. You think I don't lose sleep every time I hear Ollie's flying off to some other continent? I don't know how that doesn't affect you as well."

I bit into the sandwich I'd brought from the plane because I hadn't been hungry, and I hated to see any food go to waste. "It's hard."

"Does he still ask you to go with him?"

"Not anymore." I pushed the remainder of the sandwich away. "He understands how important my work at the sanctuary is."

We both sat there for a moment in silence, then she said, "I was disappointed that Ollie didn't put you first in his life, but you didn't put him first either. I can't say I understand it, but there's a lot about your generation I don't get."

Reana and I had become close enough over the past year that her words hurt deeply. "I've supported Ollie every step of the way."

She shrugged.

I told myself to let it go; there was nowhere good this conversation could head, but I had to know what she thought I wasn't doing. "He asked me to wait for him and that's what I've done."

Reana raised a hand in surrender. "Your relationship with my son is none of my business."

I laughed at that and some of my tension eased. "Just say it before holding it in gives you a stroke."

"That is not a funny joke," she chided. "But if you're sure you're okay with hearing what I think . . ."

I was sure I wasn't, but Reana had proven again and again how much she cared about me. We also had something strong in common—we both loved Ollie. "I am."

"I just think you'd be a whole lot happier if you accepted who you are instead of fighting against your nature."

"What's that supposed to mean?"

"You don't like to be alone, but you act like that's something shameful. You're a hard worker, but I don't think you love working at the sanctuary because it didn't end up being as social as you'd hoped it would be. You spend most of your time cleaning enclosures on your own, don't you?"

"Yes," I admitted with a slump of my shoulders.

"And you hate it."

"A little."

"So, why do you stay?"

I shrugged as the answers that came to me weren't ones I liked. "Because I chose that job over being with Ollie."

"Ah. Pride. There's a reason they say it's the root of all evil. It muddles the mind and stops people from seeing what is right before them. My husband, bless his soul, was prideful. I'm not saying he wasn't kind and generous or that I didn't love him with everything in me, but he thought he had to be perfect for me to love him back. The man couldn't balance a checkbook to save his life. He loved Driverton and felt he owed the town for being kind to us when we had no one else. And sometimes, especially at the end, he gave too much. He borrowed more than he could ever repay and tried to hide those mistakes from me. He didn't gamble. He didn't drink. He fed anyone who was hungry, but he did so with the money that would have paid our electric bill. Then placed all that weight on Ollie when he died."

"You knew?"

"Of course I did. But every time I tried to talk to Ollie about finances he would get agitated and defensive."

"Because he'd promised his father he'd keep Little Willie's open and make sure you never knew how much he'd mismanaged the money."

"I didn't know that." She inhaled sharply. "Prideful, just like I said. He shouldn't have done that. I'm not some weak woman who needs to be protected from the truth."

"Neither of them wanted to disappoint you."

"Damn fools. The only one I'm disappointed in is me for not being more vocal about how much I loved—still love both of them. Money comes and goes, jobs too. But having someone who knows your flaws and loves you anyway . . . well, that's priceless."

Just above a whisper, I said, "I don't enjoy living alone."

"No kidding," she said with a knowing smile.

I took a deep, fortifying breath. "I don't like working alone."

"The first step to having what you want is knowing what you want."

"I wish I'd said yes to going to New York with Ollie. He wanted to share all of that with me, but I wanted to prove something to myself more than I wanted to be with him."

"Sounds like you both made the same bad decision."

"Do you think he feels the same?"

"I think he's trying so hard to prove to himself he deserves you that he doesn't know what he feels. He's a good boy, though. He'll come to his senses."

After taking a sip of water, I said, "I'm going to marry your son someday, Reana. And when we have a little girl, we're going to name her after you. She'll have your grit and your fire."

She placed one hand over mine and said, "And she'll be nurturing and fill the world with love and sunshine just like her mother does."

"And probably be prideful and stubborn."

Reana laughed. "Oh, Lord."

Chapter Thirty-One

Ollie

ON THE DRIVE to Dominic's office in New York, I took the opportunity to return the call I'd received from Sophie Barrington. Even though I hadn't returned to Boston, she still checked in on me once a week. I kept her updated on my progress toward repaying Dominic and she celebrated each milestone with me without issuing the kind of warning everyone back in Driverton inevitably spouted. She shared stories of whatever shenanigans her children and grandchildren had gotten into that week. I looked forward to those uncomplicated phone calls because of the good feeling they gave me.

Although I hadn't come back from Singapore with a signed contract, the deal was moving along, and everything was pointing toward it happening by the end of the week. As soon as the paperwork was completed, Dominic would be happy, and I'd be free.

Sampling the fast-paced world of the ultra-rich had convinced me the life I wanted to build with Megan would require more balance. I didn't like being away from her as much as I was. Still, I didn't consider the last five months wasted. I could take what I'd earned, use what I'd learned, and make a good life near if not in Driverton. I'd have to travel some, but not like I'd been doing.

I was smiling as I stepped out of the elevator and checked in with Dominic's security team. He was a powerful man, but spending time around him had shown me he paid a high price for what he had. I did want to be successful, but not so successful that my family and I required bodyguards.

When his secretary let me in, Dominic motioned for me to sit while he finished looking over something on a holographic screen. He closed it with a wave of his hand then stood and walked to the front of his desk.

I rose to greet him. "Singapore is almost a done deal."

"Good. Sit."

I did. He sat on the edge of his desk and watched me with an expression I had no idea how to interpret.

He said, "You've done better than I expected. Not too many people impress me."

"Thank you."

"Which is why I feel I can trust you with a delicate matter."

"Of course. Whatever you need."

His smile was dark. "I have a problem that needs to be neutralized."

I froze. Nothing we'd ever discussed had prepared me for what sounded like he was asking me to kill someone. "Neutralized?"

"Don't worry, it's not as bad as you just imagined. All I'm asking you to do is to destroy someone's reputation, erode his connections to anyone in power, and bankrupt him. The last part isn't necessary, but I don't like to do anything halfway. I want him left with nothing."

"I don't understand."

"I think you do."

I rose to my feet. "This wasn't part of our deal."

His smile curled. "Consider this a re-negotiation of our arrangement. If you think you're successful now, I haven't begun to open doors for you. Do this and I'll owe you a favor. You have no idea what's possible for someone I'm grateful to."

Shaking my head, I took a step back. "I'm sorry but I'm not interested."

He pushed off the desk. "What if it's someone you don't like? Someone who might deserve to be taken down?"

"Like a criminal?"

"Like a man who pretends he's not one but thinks he can break any law he wants to without consequence. Bradford Wilson is a thorn in my side, and I want him removed."

A cold dread filled me. I didn't like Bradford and the reverse was undeniable, but that didn't mean I wanted to see him hurt. He'd been good to my friends. Yes, he bent and broke laws on the regular, but only with the aim of helping the innocent. He was a hero. An annoying one at times, but still someone I admired. "No," I said under my breath.

"What did you say?"

I stood taller. "No."

Dominic loomed closer. "You think you have a choice? You don't. Let me explain it to you more clearly. I have all I need to ruin Wilson. It'll happen with or without your help. But I would think very carefully before you say no to me. I could help you become one of the top ten richest men in the world. Or I could make sure no one outside of Driverton would ever hire you, not even to mow their lawns. So, what do you say?"

I didn't need time to think it over. "No. He's not perfect, but none of us are. I won't do this."

"Then you'll go down in flames with him."

I gritted my teeth and met Dominic's gaze. "So be it, but I think you'll find I'm not the only one who'll stand with him."

"The Barringtons? Ian knows better than to go up against me."

I shook my head, refusing to believe that a man who'd sat with me and mentored me on how to succeed in business also had this much evil in him.

He continued, "Or Clay Landon? If assets alone were power, I might consider him formidable, but he's never had to fight for a single thing in his life. It might be fun to see what I can dig up on him—make this a two-for-one deal. Landon loves Driverton so much, maybe I should make sure it's the only place he can afford to live."

"I won't let you do this."

"I'll enjoy watching you try to stop me."

Without answering him, I turned on my heel and strode out of his office. Something shifted inside me. Up until that meeting, I'd still been figuring out who I was and what I stood for. Saying yes to money and success had filled my life with distractions.

Saying no brought everything into sharp focus.

I knew exactly what was important and what wasn't.

Megan.

My family and friends.

My very soul.

There wasn't enough money in the world to buy my integrity or change how I treated people.

Quick on the heels of that thought was the realization I'd spent the last five months focusing on things that could never matter more than the people I loved.

I called Megan and jumped right in. "I should have chosen a goal that kept me closer to you. I should have put you first."

"Have you been talking to your mother?"

"No, why?"

"Just . . . nothing. Are you okay?"

"I am, but I have to tell you something."

"Okay."

"I love you. All it took was one look in those beautiful eyes of yours and I was a goner. You've been so patient with me, more than I deserved, but you won't have to be from now on. I'm not confused anymore. Wherever this crazy life takes us, I'm okay with it as long as we're together. Also, I might temporarily be broke again."

She laughed a little nervously. "Hold on, this is a lot to unpack. What happened?"

"The less you know, the safer you'll be—"

"No. Stop right there. I love you too. And I've done a lot of thinking about the choices *I've* made. This time, whatever we do, we do it together. Okay?"

"It could be dangerous."

"Good. We'll die together."

A laugh escaped me at that. "You don't even know what this is about."

"I don't have to. You keep talking about making a life together. Are we doing this or not?"

"We're doing it."

"Then tell me what you need and let's slay this dragon together."

And that's when I saw Megan not just as someone I wanted to care for, but as a missing piece of me. Together we were stronger.

I felt sorry for Dominic because he'd made the mistake of coming for someone from Driverton. That never ended well.

Chapter Thirty-Two

Megan

A FEW HOURS later, almost everyone was gathered at Little Willie's for what Ollie had declared a town emergency meeting. We purposefully didn't invite Bradford or Clay because Ollie said there was something he needed to say first. The room was abuzz with chatter until he raised his voice above the noise. "Everyone, before this meeting officially starts, there's something I need to say."

"You're getting married," a young man in the back yelled out.

Ollie took my hand in his and smiled down at me. "Yes, but that's not what this is about."

"Hold on," I joked. "Don't you have to ask me first?"

"We're slaying a dragon together and you already asked me if we were making a life together. Aren't we past that question?"

I slapped him playfully in the shoulder and looked around the room. "He thinks he can get out of actually proposing. Is that how things are done in Driverton?"

The booing Ollie received was mostly done in jest. Mrs. McDonald might have been serious, but she still talked to her husband, and he'd died twenty years earlier, so she might not have understood the joke.

"Or," he said with a wag of his head, "this didn't feel like the right time because I was planning to surprise you somewhere romantic with the ring I've been carrying around for months."

"You already bought the ring?" Swoon. "Can I see it?"

Smiling, he dug a small velvet box out of the breast pocket of his suit. "If I show you, I might as well ask you now."

Trying to look like fireworks weren't exploding in my heart, I said, "Only if you want to."

He began to go down onto one knee, when someone from the other side of the restaurant called out. "Don't you dare kneel down. We won't be able to see you."

He met my gaze. I nodded. He straightened then took the ring out of the box and my left hand in one of his. I froze when a thought came to me. "Wait, are my parents here?"

"We are," my mother called. People stepped out of the way and I saw she was sitting at a nearby table with Reana.

Turning back to Ollie, I said, "Okay, sorry. Keep going."

His laughter melted away any nervousness I might have had. "Megan Gassett, my father always said that the rockiest paths lead to the most beautiful places, and when I look ahead to our life together, I finally understand. Thank you for sticking with me through the tough spots and trusting that we could get here."

Maybe because the very serious reason we'd gathered everyone together was still looming, but I joked, "Did you come up with that yourself? That's romantic."

He beamed a smile at me. "I did. I've been thinking about this for a while."

"Then yes. Yes, to everything."

He slid the ring onto my finger and pulled me in for a kiss. When he raised his head, there was applause and cheers. We spent a blissful moment simply looking into each other's eyes before he said, "You ready?"

"Yes." I finally was. "Let's do this."

He turned back to the crowd. "As exciting as that was, it wasn't the reason we asked you here." He shot me a quick glance, then rolled his shoulders back and said, "I fucked up."

"Language," Reana said in exasperation.

"Is he changing his mind already?" old Mrs. McDonald asked, a few tables away.

Rumor was her bald male companion Robert had fallen in love with her in elementary school and had never given up. They were both in their eighties, inseparable, but labeled whatever they were to each other as "just friends." He said, "I can't tell, you're wearing my glasses."

I would have laughed but there was nothing funny about

what Ollie was about to share.

Ollie continued, "As you all know, I left Driverton because I wanted to make something of myself. I thought I'd found a way to, but it came with a price tag I wasn't willing to pay. And now I need your help. Someone is coming for two of our own and we need a plan for how to protect them."

Still dressed in his sheriff uniform, Tom said, "Tell us what we need to know."

"Robert," Mrs. McDonald said loudly, "take your glasses and go get my rifle."

"Easy there." Tom put a hand on Robert's shoulder and eased him down into his chair. "No one is shooting anyone until we know what's going on."

Levi joked, "Also no shooting while wearing someone else's glasses."

Ollie and I exchanged a look. This was his town, his family. He could tell them the truth. "It all started when I went away for rehab, and I got a glimpse of a world so different from ours I thought it was better. Parts were amazing." He went on to tell them about his time with the Barringtons and how kind they'd been to him. He described how unexpected Dominic's offer had been and what he'd thought would come from working with him.

The room was silent until Ollie retold the offer Dominic had made him regarding taking Bradford down and there was a collective gasp. "Of course I said no."

"That's my boy," Reana said.

"Which didn't make Corisi happy. He threatened to make it impossible for me to find work outside of Driverton. He threatened Clay as well. I'm not afraid of starting over, but we need to find a way to protect Bradford and Clay. They've done a lot for this town. There has to be something we can do for them."

"I'll call my cousin at the FBI," Everette said.

People started calling out ideas.

"Maybe you could ask him to repeat the threats, but this time record it?"

"Get the trash from outside his house. I'll look through it. That's how they find dirt on people in the movies."

"I say we just shoot him," Mrs. McDonald said.

"You could always smoochie smoochie him then threaten to share the video online."

We all stopped and looked at Everette's little sister.

She threw up her hands. "It's a thing. I've seen stories about it on TikTok."

"This isn't working. We need a real plan," I said in frustration.

"What's the problem?" Clay asked as he entered the room with Lexi at his side.

Katie answered. "Dominic asked Ollie to help him ruin Bradford. Ollie said no. Now Dominic is pissed, and we're trying to figure out how to stop a kajillionaire from ruining Ollie's life as well."

"Why didn't you come to me?" Clay asked. "I'm not afraid of Dominic."

Ollie gave my hand a squeeze. "Clay, don't underestimate him. You came up in the conversation. I don't know what he could do, but he made it sound like he could strip you of everything if you tried to help Bradford."

"And what did you say when he said that?"

"I told him I wouldn't let that happen."

"And?"

"And he said he'd enjoy watching me try to stop him."

"Is it wrong that I think that's kind of hot?" Mrs. McDonald asked.

Robert sat up straighter.

Clay exchanged a look with Lexi, then brought her hand up to his lips. "If there is one thing I've learned from all of you, it's that loyalty is worth any cost. When Dominic comes for one of us, he comes for all of us. I'll fight him until my bank account hits zero and then until my last breath if that's all I have left. Bradford has saved enough people that he deserves to have people in his life who are willing to risk it all to save him."

From the doorway, Bradford's voice boomed. "What are you talking about, Clay?"

"If people came to meetings on time, we wouldn't have to keep repeating ourselves," Mrs. McDonald said.

This time it was Clay who gave the rundown of the situation. As he spoke, Bradford's fists clenched at his sides.

When Clay finished, Bradford asked, "You meant it when you said you'd risk it all to protect me?"

"Of course," Clay said. "We're friends."

Whatever Bradford would have said next was cut off by the shock that swept through the room as Dominic entered the restaurant with a well-dressed older woman at his side.

Ollie whispered to me, "That's Sophie Barrington."

Collectively we held our breaths.

Sophie's tone was sweet but her voice carried. "I knew it. Dominic Corisi, look at how upset you have everyone. Whatever you said to poor Ollie, you need to tell him right now that you didn't mean it."

Dominic scanned the room, lingering on Bradford and Clay, then smiled. "I'll say whatever you'd like, Sophie. I've already won."

"Won?" I looked up at Ollie in confusion.

Bradford put Joanna behind him, then began to make his way toward Dominic. "You've got a lot of nerve coming in here."

Clay flanked him. "And your assessment of the situation is premature. The fight you're looking for hasn't yet begun."

"Not even close," Bradford growled.

Dominic's eyes narrowed. "So, what, you're a team now?"

Bradford and Clay exchanged a look, both nodded, then turned back to face Dominic.

To everyone's surprise, Dominic laughed. "Where's

Katie?"

"Me?" Katie asked tentatively from beside a protective Levi.

Rich or not, I had the feeling if Dominic said one wrong word to a woman in the room he wouldn't be leaving here alive. Even Ollie had a bit of a feral look in his eyes.

Dominic nodded. "Yes. You're the one who asked for this."

All eyes turned to Katie who was flashing a bright, but scared smile. "I didn't."

"Ah, but you did. Do you remember speaking to me in Florida?" Dominic folded his arms across his chest. "You wanted Bradford to realize the value of Clay's friendship but doubted I could make that happen. Clearly, you underestimated me. They're a team now."

Sophie brought a hand to her temple. "Oh, Dominic, what did you do?"

"Something people might want to be more appreciative of. There wasn't room in Driverton for two bickering billionaires. They were already putting their interests above the welfare of the town by calling attention to their presence here. It would have only been a matter of time before the people of this town paid the price for their arrogance. Now they'll remember the importance of working together."

She shook her head. "And what about Ollie? What was that about?"

"You know I don't work with anyone I don't trust. I had

to know if he could be bought." Dominic met Bradford's glare. "Ollie might not like you, but there was nothing I could bribe nor threaten him with that made him willing to betray you. And I dug deep into my dark side to scare him. He didn't budge. You're welcome."

Bradford looked to Ollie for confirmation. Ollie nodded humbly. When he turned back to Dominic, Bradford snarled, "You're a real piece of work, you know that? You're lucky this was a game because if you had actually threatened Ollie the last thing you'd see is *my* dark side."

Sophie raised both hands. "We should probably go."

Reana said, "Wait." She rose from her seat and made her way over to stand in front of Dominic. "You owe not only my son an apology, but Bradford and Clay as well."

Dominic's eyes narrowed.

Her hands went to her hips. "Don't make me call your mother."

Without missing a beat, he said, "My mother let me believe she was dead while she hid from my father for years. She doesn't exactly lecture me."

Reana's mouth rounded. "Oh, that explains a lot." Then she pressed her lips together. "But that still doesn't excuse poor manners." She tapped a foot impatiently. "Well?"

Between gritted teeth, he said, "No one was ever actually in danger of losing anything."

"Mr. Corisi, do you know what the difference between a hero and a villain is?"

He neither nodded nor shook his head.

She continued, "The difference between me keeping this old lady sandal on my foot or taking it off and whooping your ass with it."

Both Ollie and I choked back laughter because we both knew she meant it.

Dominic seemed to as well. His expression softened. "There's nothing more beautiful than a mama bear defending her cub. I never had that, but I respect it when I see it." He nodded toward Ollie. "Ollie, I may have taken things too far with you. It won't happen again."

I nudged Ollie until he said, "Apology accepted."

Dominic looked back and forth between Bradford and Clay then flashed them both a smile. "It's almost a shame none of this was real. I've retired from that life and can't say I don't miss it sometimes. But I do apologize for upsetting your friends."

Sophie added, "And don't forget all the hard work Ollie put into the deal you made with him."

Dominic met Ollie's gaze. "Singapore signed. You did it. You matched the money I invested in you so it's yours to keep."

"I don't want your money," Ollie said.

My eyes rounded.

Reana gave her son an intense look.

Even Pete, someone who hardly spoke in large groups, said, "You might want to rethink that, son."

Ollie looked down into my eyes. "I confused having more with being more and I won't make that mistake again. You and I will have an incredible life together with or without that money."

My love for him had me swaying toward him. "I know we will."

"I'll only take it if you think I should."

I thought about his father's pride and how much it had cost Ollie. I also thought about Ollie's desire to continue to take care of people. Dominic wasn't giving him money; Ollie had earned it. "I can't wait to see all the good you do with it."

He bent and kissed me quickly, before turning back to Dominic. "I'll take the money because I earned it, but I want to renegotiate the terms."

Dominic folded his arms across his chest again and waited.

I knew exactly what Ollie was going to say before he even began to voice it, and I hugged him tight because my man was a genius. "The deal between us won't be complete until you've brought your family here and shared a meal with us. Here or at my mother's house."

"What?" Ollie's request was not what Dominic had been expecting.

"You heard me. You don't work with people you don't trust. I don't take money from people I don't know. You made some hasty assumptions about us, but Driverton is a place where you can make a mistake, even a very public one, and still be accepted. We're not good at keeping secrets, but we also don't hold grudges. Come and spend some time with us. See what Bradford and Clay are building here. You won't need your security. Almost everyone here is packing." The sound of guns being placed on tables echoed through the room. "Except for Mrs. McDonald, because she really wants to shoot someone lately and her sight is going."

Johanna nudged Bradford, who frowned at her until she nudged him again. He growled then said, "You're also welcome to visit our mini-horse rescue."

Clay's smile turned light and easy. "Dominic, life is too short to be angry all the time. When you come back, we'll talk. Have you considered goat yoga?"

"Or investing in a turtle sanctuary right here in Driverton," I said spontaneously.

Dominic's attention snapped to me. "A turtle sanctuary?"

I smiled up at Ollie. "When an opportunity arises, you have to shoot your shot, right?"

He kissed me and chuckled. "Go get him, Turtle Lady." Then he hugged me close. "Not that we don't have the money to do it ourselves, but I like the way you think. Investors are always a good thing."

Dominic looked around at all the smiling faces and said, "I don't understand this town."

"That's the point," Ollie said.

I cuddled against Ollie. "I felt the same in the beginning then I fell in love with every single part of it."

"And it fell right back in love with you," Ollie said, kissing the top of my head.

Chapter Thirty-Three

>>>><<<<

Ollie

LATER THAT NIGHT, in a hotel room near Driverton, I woke to a naked Megan snuggled to my side. The diamond I'd put on her finger sparkled in the dim light of the lamp we'd forgotten to turn off.

Her eyes fluttered open. "You awake?"

I kissed her forehead. "Yeah."

"We set out to slay a dragon together, but we did something better—we tamed it. I'm kind of proud of us."

I smiled. "We had help, but I'm glad it worked out the way it did."

"I've been thinking about the future. Are you okay with living at least part-time in Driverton?"

"More than part-time."

"Then we should start saving up for a house. How much money did Dominic invest in you?"

"A hundred million."

She sat straight up. "What? OMG! I had no idea it was

that much."

"What kind of money did you think we were talking about?"

"I don't know—a couple thousand dollars?"

"A bit more than that."

"Yeah." She settled against me again. "Hold on, does that mean you have a hundred million dollars?"

"No, it means we do."

"We could not only afford a house but make our own turtle sanctuary."

"Yes, we could."

"And employ people from Driverton."

"We do need jobs in the area. If the facility is nice enough, it could also double as a cover for why rich people visit."

"To support turtle conservation."

"Exactly."

"You could run the business side of it while I handle recruitment, training, and outreach."

"That sounds perfect. I may also do some consulting on the side. Sophie's son Asher heard about my success in Singapore and wants to hear about how I made it happen. I'll tell them everything I learned for no charge, but if they think I know something of value, someone else might as well."

She raised her head and looked down into my eyes. "This time if you move away I'm going with you."

"You damn sure are, although I'm not going anywhere. Short trips, yes. I've seen the world out there and I like Driverton a whole lot more."

"I love you," she declared before kissing me deeply.

Only once she was cuddled back to my side, did I have a chance to say, "I love you too."

"We should invite Dominic to our wedding," she said out of the blue.

I chuckled. "Sure. I don't know if he'll come, but I'll be inviting the Barringtons so what's one more billionaire?"

"Inviting him to dinner at your mom's was genius."

"I thought so."

"Do you think his wife knows what he did?"

"I don't know, but I bet he'll be grateful if we don't tell her."

Sure, that last thought wasn't my kindest, but Dominic had taught me well.

It was time he learned that in Driverton being friends didn't mean we didn't give each other shit. In fact, if he thought we were done with him just because he'd apologized, he had a lot to learn about small town folks.

We didn't hold grudges.

But we did like to get even.

THE END

Don't miss a release, a sale or a bonus scene. Sign up for my newsletter today.

forms.aweber.com/form/58/1378607658.htm

More books By Ruth Cardello

The Legacy Collection:
Maid for the Billionaire
For Love or Legacy
Bedding the Billionaire
Saving the Sheikh
Breaching the Billionaire: Alethea's Redemption

The Andrades:
Come Away with Me
Home to Me
Maximum Risk
Somewhere Along the Way
Loving Gigi

The Barrington Billionaires:
Always Mine
Stolen Kisses
Trade it All
A Billionaire for Lexi (Novella with two bonus novellas)
Let it Burn
More than Love
Forever Now
Never Goodbye

Reluctantly Alpha
Reluctantly Rescued
Reluctantly Romanced
Loving a Landon
Loathing a Landon
Everette: Driverton 1
Levi: Driverton 2
Ollie: Driverton 3

The Westerlys Series:
In the Heir
Up for Heir
Royal Heir
Hollywood Heir
Runaway Heir

Corisi Billionaires:
The Broken One
The Wild One
The Secret One

The Lost Corisis:
He Said Always
He Said Never
He Said Together
He Said Forever

The Switch Series:
Strictly Business

Out of Love

Twin Find Series:
Strictly Family
Out of Office

Bachelor Tower Series:
Insatiable Bachelor
Impossible Bachelor
Undeniable Bachelor

Lone Star Burn Series:
Taken, Not Spurred
Tycoon Takedown
Taken Home
Taking Charge

Temptation Series:
Untouchable Kate

About the Author

Ruth Cardello was born the youngest of 11 children in a small city in southern Massachusetts. She spent her young adult years moving as far away as she could from her large extended family. She lived in Boston, Paris, Orlando, New York—then came full circle and moved back to New England. She now happily lives one town over from the one she was born in. For her, family trumped the warmer weather and international scene.

She was an educator for 20 years, the last 11 as a kindergarten teacher. When her school district began cutting jobs, Ruth turned a serious eye toward her second love—writing and has never been happier. When she's not writing, you can find her chasing her children around her small farm, riding her horses, or connecting with her readers online.

Contact Ruth:
Website: RuthCardello.com
Email: RCardello@RuthCardello.com
FaceBook: Author Ruth Cardello
Twitter: @RuthieCardello

Made in the USA
Monee, IL
19 July 2025